A FEATHER'S WORTH

SPAWN OF DARKNESS

S. A. PARKER

A Feather's Worth (Spawn of Darkness Series)

Copyright © S. A. Parker, all rights reserved.

This series is a work of fiction. Any resemblance to characters and situations is purely coincidental and not intended by the author.

❦ Created with Vellum

CONTENTS

NOTE FROM THE AUTHOR   v

Chapter 1   1
Chapter 2   11
Chapter 3   24
Chapter 4   32
Chapter 5   43
Chapter 6   59
Chapter 7   68
Chapter 8   75
Chapter 9   84
Chapter 10   99
Chapter 11   110
Chapter 12   125
Chapter 13   138
Chapter 14   152

Acknowledgments   161
About the Author   163
Spawn of Darkness Series   165

NOTE FROM THE AUTHOR

First and foremost, Dell is a sex slave. Some of the situations that occur in A Feather's Worth are brutal, but integral to her character development and the story arc. The circumstances she finds herself in are significantly darker than A Token's Worth.

If you struggle with darker elements please put this book down **now** ... you have been warned. Everyone else? Buckle up!

Sterling
Kingdom of The Lord Almighty
Varian
Sun God Territory Lines
Neutral Stone
The East
Herdsworth
Grueling
Hind Meadow
The Village of Noft
The Desert of Lai
The Ruins of Bane
Kygole
Day
Dusk
Dawn
Night

For Mum and Nana.
Thank you for showing me the true value of a woman's worth.

CHAPTER ONE

I draw a deep breath. The movement tugs at my flayed skin and I exhale with a shuddering groan. Fucking cat-o-nine.

The breath sends a swirl of dust mites into my nostrils and I have only a split second to brace myself before I sneeze nose jizz all over my rotten mattress. I heave in pain as a warm spill of blood drools down my back and pools on my already bloodied mattress.

"Shut your pie hole! Nobody said you could groan!"

I squeeze my eyes shut. Ballsack One is in full downer mode since his pal went for a nap. He doesn't like hanging around on his own. He prefers the company of Ballsack Two as he whines and bitches about being stuck in my little cell, standing guard over my shredded body. It's a bit excessive if you ask me—assigning me two guards when I can't even lift my arm to flick this curl out of my mouth. It's been stuck in there for hours, days … whatever. Coating my tongue. Tangling through my teeth. It's really fucking annoying.

I heave another breath, repressing the urge to groan again

as my skin tugs and pulls at odd and unnatural angles. I don't have to look at it myself to know I'm in pieces.

Outside.

Inside.

It's almost fitting that I'm here—back in my little room, the darkness.

My girls ...

Fuck.

The door creaks open and Kroe strides in carrying a small jar and a bowl of something fragrant, a heavy frown fracturing his face. His features are embossed with shadows, his chest bare, black pants slung low on his hips revealing the tapered sculpt of his torso. He assesses me, brown eyes smouldering, canines glistening in the flickering lantern light. He lets out a low grumble that has Ballsack One standing like he has a rod up his arse.

"You haven't touched her, have you?"

Ballsack One pales. "No, sir! Of course not!"

Kroe hisses at the fucker. "Her skin's bleeding again. Explain that? And be quick about it, before I slice your knob clean off."

Yikes. I know he'll do it, so does Ballsack One by the way his hands drop to his crotch. I don't blame him for shielding his party prodder.

"The slut has an allergy to the dust. Every time she sneezes, she bleeds everywhere. *Sir.*"

Kroe assesses him slowly, glacial gaze shifting back to me. "Not even a finger up her twat?"

Ballsack One shakes his head. "No, sir."

Kroe nods, sniffing at the space around us, no doubt scenting the thick aroma of male sex juices staining the air right now, though it still doesn't mask the scent of the seven years I spent in this cold, dark room. That shit's potent. A stain on the space that will probably always be there.

Ballsack One and Two have been showering me with their cock cream ever since I was dumped in their care. The pasty, leering bastards stand over me, breathing heavily while I pretend to be asleep, trying not to gag every time I get bathed in another hot load of cum.

"Just don't cum on her back while you're fantasising over her arse." Kroe prowls towards me, places the bowl and jar on the blood-stained ground and sits on the edge of my bed.

Ballsack One shakes his head enthusiastically, shoulders loosening. "No, sir. Sorry, sir. Thank you, sir."

Fucking pussy. I can see him trembling from here, probably worried he'll get castrated for spurting all over me. He has no idea Kroe gets off on that shit.

I know Kroe well. Sometimes, I feel like I know the bastard better than I know myself.

"Get the fuck out, and close the door behind you. Wait on the other side until I'm done." The air of authority in Kroe's voice is potent, and I let out a trembling breath. Because this … this is the man who took my virginity. This is the man who anchored me to the darkness, taught me to fuck. Taught me to love … in some messed up capacity.

Ballsack One scurries out of the room like a cockroach hell bent on dodging the boot. Kroe smirks and straightens his shoulders, probably reaffirming himself of the metaphorical size of his cock. It doesn't take much with him. It's like a drug, something he's hooked on.

Something he *thrives* on.

Cool hands skim my flayed skin and I hiss through my teeth, chewing through the pain. He pulls the rogue curl from my mouth. If my vagina were still functioning, I'd have orgasmed on the spot.

"You're not healing as quickly as you usually do, Cupcake. Have they been touching you without my permission? You can tell me …"

The sixteen-year-old me would probably be swooning over that question, trying to convince herself he cares for her on a deeper level. The twenty-three-year-old me knows better. I *know* he cares about me on a deeper level. But he cares in all the wrong ways. For all the wrong reasons.

Are the coffers suffering since I've been away, Kroe? I bet they fucking are.

Still, the comment has a lingering effect on my fucked up, frolicking heart, because here we are, back in my room that smells like all the shit he's done to me over the years …

There was a time when I knew little more than these four walls, the darkness, and the man seated beside me. Though I didn't know it at the time, I realise it now, recognise it in the beast coiled within me … more than one monster was forged in this room.

I shake my head, no. They haven't been touching me. Doesn't mean they don't want to. Doesn't mean I haven't smelt their desire, thick and musky with the lingering scent of their urge to dominate me.

"Good … that's good." He prods me in a particularly tender spot and I tense, sucking air through my nose, causing me to sneeze so hard another warm spill of blood trickles down the sides of my back.

Kroe puffs out a huff as I breathe through the pain, trying to cling to my flailing composure. "You're a mess."

No shit.

He shifts his body, washing his scent over me as he sinks his hand into his pocket and tugs out a white handkerchief. I close my eyes, scrunching them shut, and very nearly fucking wail as he dabs my wounds before tossing the bloodied, sodden material onto the floor. Taking the lid off the jar, he dips his finger into the translucent substance.

"I'm going to smear some ointment on your back. I don't

want to risk you getting an infection after I went to so much trouble to get you back."

That stings. Not the ointment, he hasn't gotten there yet. I'm talking about the thought of my girls, up on that dais, backs being splayed open ... dying.

My fault.

My fucking fault.

My beast coils within herself—poor, frightened little thing. I reach inside myself and stroke her. She doesn't purr, even though I have fucking fantastic petting skills thank you very much, but I sense her loosening up a little.

Good. I have a feeling I'm going to need her before I leave this world to their shit.

Kroe dabs the cool substance across my back. It bites, but I *revel* in the pain. Because I deserve this.

I fucking deserve this.

Kroe whistles a tune, one I haven't heard before, as those familiar fingers paint my skin with something that will only prolong the inevitable ... because us girls? We're destined for a life of pain. Suffering. Torment.

Then we die.

It's predictable. Inevitable. Unchangeable.

"Now, Cupcake ..." He dips his finger into the jar again, before continuing his painful administrations. I'm biting my tongue so hard it's bleeding. "After I finish this, I'm going to feed you some broth. You're going to slurp it back as eagerly as you gulp my cum, or else I'll give one of the other girls a taste of that cat-o-nine."

I want to tell him to go fuck himself, but I just don't have the heart. Or the voice. Or the breath. And I *am* hungry ... thirsty ...

Kroe replaces the lid to the jar—his fingers smeared in bloody, translucent goo. He proceeds to wipe his fingers on his pants and assesses me, brow creasing. I know what's coming. I want to plead for mercy, to beg for him to let me wither into a moisture-less husk.

He stands and tugs at my legs one at a time, persuading them off the edge of the bed. They land with heavy thumps, leaving me at an odd angle for a few heavy moments, my body seizing up from fear with the thought of moving another inch. Kroe wraps his fingers around my shoulders, his large hands almost swallowing them whole, and pulls.

A shrill yell escapes my parched lips as my composure finally corrodes. He sits me on the edge of the bed, wiping the sweat from my brow despite the cool chill to the room.

"That hurt, didn't it?"

Wincing, I nod my response. Yes, it fucking hurt, you bastard.

"Calm down, Cupcake. Deep breaths…"

Inwardly cursing the fucker, I do as he says, because I know it's the right thing to do. Unless I want to pass out and fall face first into his crotch.

"That's it… deep breaths. You're doing well."

Breathe in my nose, out through my mouth. Repeat. Try not to focus on the warmth pooling around my arse. It's not pee… well, I hope it's not. I'm pretty sure it's blood. I'm not sure how much more of it I can afford to lose. And to be honest, dying in this place would *actually* be the worst way to go. Much worse than being eaten by a giant, Fae-eating penis serpent. For me, anyway.

My gaze drops to Kroe's shoes, highly polished and decorated with iron studs. They reek of whore money.

He reaches down for the bowl, back muscles rippling with the movement, then crouches next to the bed and drags the spoon through the creamy broth, before bringing it up to my mouth.

It smells good … I'll admit. But honestly, at this point, I'd probably eat a fucking rock. I'm that bloody hungry.

"Open, Cupcake. You've caused enough damage as it is, don't you think?" Kroe likes to twist the knife when he knows you're vulnerable.

My mouth trembles, cracked lips crumbling as I slowly open my mouth, push my heavy tongue through my teeth, and wait. Always the patient little whore.

Kroe smirks, eyes glimmering as he skims the spoon along my tongue and pours the tepid liquid down my throat. I choke it back like the pro I am, then open my mouth for more, tongue hanging out like a pauper begging for a penis token.

He chuckles. I don't have to be a genius to understand why he's amused. I know exactly what he's picturing as he drags off another load of the creamy broth and pours it down my throat.

I needed this. I don't even care that it looks like cum. That it's dribbling down my chin, splattering onto my breasts and making a filthy mess.

That I look like an animal right now. That I'm being treated like one.

Kroe drops the spoon in the bowl and readjusts the waistband of his pants. "That's it …" His cock twitches, pressing against the firm material of his pants as he lifts the spoon and pours another load down my throat.

The bastard's getting off on this, though I'm not surprised. It doesn't stop me from poking out my tongue again. The more I drink, the more I realise how depleted my body is.

Smirking, he trickles another spoonful over my face. A small sound escapes me as I chase the residue with my tongue.

Kroe growls, from deep within his chest. "That's what I like to see, Cupcake. You know how I like it."

No, I'm just fucking parched.

He doesn't plunge me with his penis, though he's clearly fantasising about it as he spoons the rest of the broth down my throat, tight pants nursing his throbbing erection.

I'm appreciative—because it would probably kill me right now. Not to mention the fact that my vagina is in a super comatose state. To be honest, I'm scared to even try and wake the bitch. I know she's mad at me. She doesn't think logically when she's mad, spitting her juices over things that the sensical part of my brain doesn't find remotely fascinating.

Still though, I hope she isn't dead down there. The thought of wading through a toiling river of inevitable fuckery with a dead vagina is worrying to say the least. I need the bitch if I'm going to survive this long enough to make amends. If. My chances are looking slim. Especially considering Kroe has me under twenty-four-hour surveillance.

I yearn to see my Sun Gods, even for a short time. I wish I could apologise to them for prolonging their access to a power-boost. Not that I deserve their godly attention right now. What a shitty rebel I turned out to be—there's probably over twenty girls upstairs either missing limbs or nursing their own flayed skin because of me.

My fault.

Kroe sets the bowl on the ground, before easing me back onto the bed, face down, arse exposed.

He turns to leave, padding a few footsteps towards my door before turning back to face me. "I'm glad to have you back. Though next time you decide to run, perhaps you'll think of the other girls' wellbeing before you go. Not that I intend on letting you out of my sight, but if you find a way to leave again, I won't be so lenient with my punishments."

I swallow the lump in my throat as a wave of regret washes through me, twisting my naked heart.

My fault.

Even if I wanted to, I wouldn't leave here again—not without my girls.

I couldn't.

He spins and exits. Ballsack One and Two stride back into my room, closing the door behind them and pressing themselves against the damp wall, covering several depictions of my mother while they shamelessly ogle my arse, the scent of arousal thickening in the air about us.

Guess I can't blame them, they're in direct view of my arse and have nothing better to look at. I just wish I could cover up my star sandwich, otherwise I'm going to get tossed between two leering Ballsacks who *think* they can control their impulses. Who think they can resist.

They can't. I can see it in their eyes, the potential to break. And it's not going to be pretty for any of us, because Kroe doesn't like to be … defied.

Oh … shit.

Sucking in a deep, shuddering breath, I almost groan as I'm struck with an idea. The beginnings of a plan.

It's not much yet, and it's risky, but I know Kroe about as well as he knows my delicate inner workings. That's his weakness, his *one* fucking weakness …

Me.

No matter how low I've stooped in the past, I've always survived. Because of Kroe.

He wouldn't kill me—I'm certain of it. But if he thinks I'm a flight hazard again? Perhaps he'll keep me close. Closer than normal.

I know what that means—more fuckery at the hands of Kroe. The thought makes me want to vomit up my milky spoof broth. But it's not about me anymore, it's about everyone I've let down, and there are too many of them to count.

It's time to face my demons. My shadows. The darkness inside me.

It's time to tame my beast.

Kroe needs to die … and I need to be the one to do it.

CHAPTER TWO

*I*t's come. The inevitable.
I knew it would. That it would sneak up and seek to destroy me. I dreaded it. Feared it even.

It's torn me up on the inside while I've done everything in my power to fight it. Stretched me farther than I ever thought possible. Pushed my boundaries … my limits.

Tormented me.

Sweat is collecting on my brow as I fight against my body's impulses. But I'm fighting a losing battle. I know the fucker is going to win.

I need to pee.

It's the first time since I got slashed open, probably because I've lost so much blood. If I don't let it loose soon, I think I'll actually die. But making it all the way over to that chamber pot in the corner there might just kill me anyway.

Fuck you, bladder. Why can't you be comatose like my wayward fucking vagina.

This is going to be humiliating with an audience of two leering Ballsacks. Me, butt naked, back in tatters as I squat in the corner and moan like a menstruating drako from the pain.

Great. Just fucking great.

"It's looking pretty bleak to me," B-One drawls.

"No shit." B-Two scuffs at the stone floor with his boot, flicking a lock of icy blonde hair from his eyes. "Fucking breeders' fault, if you ask me. Not doing their job right."

B-One nods, running his tongue over his lips, widening his stance and peering at my arsehole for the millionth time today. "Agreed."

They've been bleating about the lack of women for the past few hours. Apparently it's a real vagina drought—there just isn't enough to go around. Probably because they keep tearing out our uteruses or cutting off our heads.

But no. Of course, they would blame the breeders.

I wiggle my hips to stem the urge to pee. Even in her non-functioning state, my vagina's proving to be a bitch. All I'm asking from her is that she keeps those golden gates closed until my fucking back heals. She's such a pain in my whore-arse.

"At least there's plenty of tail here to keep us entertained." B-One cocks his head to the side to gain a better viewing angle of my wiggly hips. "I think she needs to pee."

Yeah, no shit, testicle chin.

My vagina almost lets the flood gates come crashing down, for no other reason besides the fact that she's hell bent on dragging me to the grave with her. Screw this.

I pull my knee under my body, hissing like a feline mid-mate, and tug my other leg under too. A warm spill of blood rolls off my back as I stretch my scabs out over the sharp bones, repressing the urge to scream.

"This should be interesting..."

Wanker.

Trembling, I manoeuvre myself off the bed, all my bits out on display as I hobble stoically towards my rusty old chamber pot in the corner, dribbles of blood trailing my path … drip, drip, drip.

"Did you hear another one died?"

My ears perk right up, though I hide my intrigue like a good little hoe.

"No … infection?"

"Think so. She was a sweet little piece of arse, too. Unfortunate." B-Two gestures towards me, half squatting over my chamber pot while trying to keep my back as straight as possible. Don't want to piss all over the ground and give these cocksuckers something else to squirt over.

"It's a shame they don't all heal as well as this bitch."

Something I'm not doing very well at right now, because my vagina just dropped the golden gates and at the same time, my body heaved forward in automatic, cataclysmic relief, opening my wounds and sending blood dribbling down my legs.

"He can't afford to lose many more from this batch. How many did we bring back? Seventy-three?"

I almost tip over at that. As it is, I lose my footing and end up with one-foot ankle deep in my goddamn chamber pot. I groan inwardly—partially from the pain, partially from the piss I'm semi-marinating in … but mainly from the news that Kroe's been out recruiting more vaginas to fill his whore castle.

I pull my foot out and tentatively shake the pee off. It makes me think of Drake and Kal, landing me in piss to keep the men on the streets at bay. My heart drops into my stomach.

I need to keep it together, let them go. They can't get me here anyway, because the wards would kill my Sun Gods if anybody noticed them defying the King's idea of a 'perfect society'.

"Seventy-four. There's only twenty-two left from that hoard, though. Mainly because that group of them drowned themselves in straight grog. Stupid bitches. Why anyone would want to die choking on their own vomit voluntarily, beats me."

My lips are trembling … so is my chin. My left eye is twitching and I'm struggling to contain my composure as I slowly, painfully hobble back to my pathetic excuse for a bed. But most importantly? My beast is peering out at these two Ballsacks, watching them with guarded curiosity from her place curled tightly inside me.

She's been so fragile, so tentative … refusing to entertain my advances to lure her out of her state of misery. But now her tail is flicking back and forth, and she just licked her fucking chops … I think these fucktards have finally piqued her interest.

Good … because I can't do this on my own, and I wasn't too keen on dragging the bitch out by the scruff of her neck when she's looking so bedraggled.

"Sometimes I think it's good when they take themselves out," B-Two drawls. "There's no point in them once they forget their place in this world. Wasted space, only good for a wrestle."

B-One shrugs. "Personally, I prefer the ones that put up a bit of a fight. Makes it more exciting."

Letting out a shuddering breath, I give my beast a little stroke—purely to encourage the way she's leering at the two testicles over there as I gently lower myself onto the mattress.

She's here.
She's with me.
We've got this.

Twelve days later

"I've had to stand here staring at that round arse for the past two weeks, it's not fair. She looks ripe for fucking to me. What's the use of her if you can't screw the hoe?" B-One drawls, voice thick and rusty. It makes him sound a lot sexier than he is.

"Kroe's just trying to tighten her cunt. He did go to a lot of trouble to get the slag back."

Slag? Really, B-Two? That's the best you could come up with? I thought better of you, I really did.

No, wait. That's a lie.

My expectations weren't particularly high to start with, and he certainly hasn't done anything since to remedy that factor. Neither has. Unfortunately for them.

"If I had a bitch with an arse like that, I'd want to keep her on a short leash too, so I could nestle myself balls deep into her tight little arsehole whenever I felt like it."

I want to gag but I'm pretending to be asleep. Besides, this is progress—we're actually getting somewhere. Finally.

"Nah, I want to put my cock between those lips of hers, fuck her wayward mouth so hard she's choking on me, then fill her guts with so much cum the bitch thinks she's pregnant."

The other one chuckles, and then they're both cackling away. Their way of wanking each other off.

I hear this conversation a lot. It's really fucking repetitive, just like the sound of water dripping in the corner of my room.

Drip.

Drip.

Drip.

My back's almost entirely healed. I know because it's itching like a motherfucker—probably mottled with hundreds of new scars. I don't mind, they tell my story and hide a multitude of sins.

I breathe in the scent of my old, stagnant, bloody mattress. It's really seen some shit. If it could talk, hell, it would have some tales…

But it can't, and it doesn't. It just has dust … lots and lots of fucking dust.

The sneezing continued to tear open my wounds, prolonging my healing process. It gave me plenty of time to soothe the beast inside me. To gain her trust. It also gave these two Ballsacks plenty of opportunities to dig their own graves.

Drip.

Drip.

Drip …

Moist fucking hole in the roof, I wish it would stop leaking its juices everywhere. It never used to do this.

Actually…

Sweet baby courtesan.

The leaky pipe in the bathing chamber on the ground floor … fuck me, this room must be directly below it!

I roll my eyes to the side and stare upwards, at the square of stone a slightly different shade to the rest of the ceiling. Water pools around the edges, gathering in the corners. Fat droplets fall to the floor.

Drip.

Drip.

Drip.

I picture the communal bathing chamber above, the layout of the room. There, at the base of the scum lined central pool and directly above my room, lies a large mat, tattered, filthy, edges frayed and torn … it's covering a fucking trapdoor!

A second direct route to my room … perhaps precaution in the event the main access off his personal quarters on the second floor was blocked.

A way out … or another way in.

Drip.

Drip.

Drip.

Closing my eyes, I start to formulate a plan, but it's intricate. Not to mention it's going to take some time and cooperation from at least *one* of the other girls. Though they'd no longer see me as a survivor … as one of them.

Not after seeing this room.

I suck in a laboured breath. Focus on my plan. This is not about me, this is about the girls I've let down.

I'm going to need an iron fucking labia, because it's going to take some guts with a side of impulsive bitch to carry out what I have in mind.

I snap my eyes open, body on high alert as B-One slips a hand between my crack and strokes my arsehole with his thumb. How do I know it's his thumb? He's groping at my vagina at the same time, and he's not being gentle about it.

Burying my head in the mattress, I grip a handful of the torn material. I can see where this is going. Surely it's just as uncomfortable for them when they go in dry?

"You like that, bitch?" he seethes, kneading my curls, tugging hard against my scalp and pulling my face from the mattress.

No, I don't like that, because my vagina's either dead in her ditch somewhere or she's up and abandoned me, so I'm not even going to get any kind of sick pleasure from this little stunt.

B-Two makes his way into my line of sight, pants around

his knees while he pumps his chode to the vision of B-One fondling my arsehole. But then his hand retreats for all of two point three seconds as he spreads my cheeks wide, before he sheathes himself balls deep.

I scream, I can't help it, because it hurts as much as you would expect.

He thrusts into me, parting my arse cheeks further, giving him full access to my pucker. My hips are rising off the bed with the motion, my neck cranked at an odd angle.

B-Two's getting agitated, he's broken a sweat and spittle's flying from between his gritted teeth. His hand just isn't doing the job, because it's my mouth he's after. My mouth he's *verbally fantasized* about.

The beast inside me cracks a lazy eye open, licks her fucking chops and purrs. I get the feeling she likes playing with her food. Guess we're going to find out because I'm about to set the bitch loose.

I swallow the bile rising in my throat as he tugs at me roughly, pulling me to my hands and knees.

"Take my cock, slag." He thrusts his firm, weepy cock at my mouth.

A strangled sound escapes me as he pries my teeth open with fumbling fingers and plunges it in, hard and deep.

My beast positions herself on her haunches, tail flicking from side to side, readying herself to pounce. She's even drooling. Crude creature.

I hold her down as he thrusts, gaining his rhythm to the beat of B-One plunging away behind me. I have to time this perfectly for full impact, let her loose at the *ideal* moment. Don't want a half-cocked job…

His penis becomes firmer, the veins pulsing against the sensitive flesh inside my mouth. I roll my tongue to send him over the edge, and he tumbles, moaning as he begins to empty his load deep down my fucking throat.

I unleash my beast.

She pounces, my jaw clamping down as she sinks my canines into the fleshy meat of his pulsing cock, blood oozing from my mouth. He bellows, the air becoming potent with his fear.

My arse is suddenly empty, the door to my cell swinging open as B-One dashes from the room.

This cock is really fucking chewy—even my beast is having trouble getting through that thing, but she's determined to do me proud. Meanwhile, B-Two is clawing at us with his hands, shrieking and pleading and generally being a fucking nuisance ... but my beast's not letting go. Having finally made it through the flesh, sinew and cum tract—we rise, leaning back and sitting delicately on our legs folded beneath us as we watch B-Two writhe on the floor, holding his bloodied stump of a knob and gushing blood all over the floor of my room.

My beast spits the severed cock onto the ground in front of him, wearing a smile dripping with blood that I'm sure looks fucking savage.

She winks at him. "You told me to take your cock."

He screams louder, before passing out on the ground, just as I rein my beast the hell in.

Fuck.

Smile gone, I'm panting, trembling all over. I bring my ruby stained hands to my face and study them, smothered in the blood of this man I likely just killed—by chewing off his penis.

Holy fucking hell.

On the upside, now I don't feel so bad about having my uterus sliced from my body.

On the downside, I just bit a man's cock off. Well, part of me did. How prevalent that part of me is, I have no idea ... I just know it felt fucking amazing at the time.

But now ... now I hate myself.

Gagging, I cover my mouth with my hand, swallowing hard. But saliva continues to fill my mouth, tongue tingling until I can't contain the urge any longer. I vomit bile all over the Ballsack passed out on the ground with half a bleeding cock.

Kroe runs into the room, panting, followed by a ghostly white B-One. They survey the carnage around me.

I finish heaving my meagre guts up and Kroe clears his throat, straightens the lines of his immaculate suit and slicks his shiny hair back with the palm of his hand. "Did you tell anybody else about this on your way to collect me?"

The one remaining Ballsack shakes his head like his life fucking depends on it. "No, sir. I came straight to you. I thought you'd want to deal with the bitch yourself."

Kroe nods, rubbing his finger and thumb along the base of his jaw. "Right. Good." He turns, pushing the door shut and locking it from the inside before reaching inside his jacket.

I know what's coming, so does my beast. She's perched high, straining against the bonds I have over her, fighting for a front row seat. I wouldn't be surprised if she puts her little feral paw up and asks for fucking popcorn.

Kroe spins so swiftly I barely catch a glimpse of the blade as it swipes through the throat of Ballsack One, sending blood cascading down his front. He grabs at the shredded flesh over his jugular, gasping for breath.

What a shit way to die.

Kroe turns his back on me, plunging the blade into the chest of the other Ballsack, who's likely already dead from blood loss.

Strangely, my full body shakes have ceased and a smile is curling my lips. I realise my beast is salivating at the thought of rolling around in the puddle of blood on the ground that's almost large enough to bathe in.

So unladylike.

I rein the barbaric bitch in and the trembling renews its vigour.

Kroe prowls towards me, that fine suit that was so perfect a moment ago now spattered in blood. He's panting his bloodlust away with each breath, a gleam in his eyes ...

One I recognise.

One I was *banking* on.

Stopping, he peers down his nose at me.

He backhands me across my cheek, so hard that I fight to hold consciousness.

Fucking *ouch*.

He seethes through his elongated canines. "You stupid, stupid girl."

My beast has abandoned me; pussy. Though Kroe doesn't realise it, I think he has her on a leash.

Perhaps he *does* realise it.

"What do you say?" he asks, tipping my chin back with his index finger. I'm meeting him eye to eye—all six and a half feet of him.

"Sorry," I croak, knowing it will be enough.

He nods. "Good girl. Keep those teeth to yourself or else I'll pull them out of your fucking jaw before taking a girl's head for every tooth taken. Do you understand?"

I swallow back the residue of bile coating my mouth, hard to do when your neck's so strained. "I understand."

"Good," he repeats, undoing his zipper and tugging his erect self free of his trousers. "Now, open up that pretty mouth of yours."

I do.

I know this man intimately ... too intimately. I knew he'd want to pump his own power lust by dipping himself into the jaws of death ... claiming me. Right now, I could sink my teeth in, chew his cock right off and spit it on the ground next to that lonely one over there—looking like a giant, bloody slug.

But he knows I won't.

I'll find another way to do it ... something not so drawn out and brutal. Something not so ... personal.

Not only that, my beast is cowering somewhere in the shadows over there, as Kroe thrusts his familiar length down my throat like he's plunging a bogged toilet. She wants nothing to do with this. Nothing to do with my plan. I don't blame her. I just hope she'll grow a pair when I need her to.

Then it hits me ...

I played those two men like a couple of penis fiddles.

I *knew* this would happen, with every fibre of my being.

Knew it from the moment I woke on this crusty old bed, broken and bloody under the watchful eyes of two leering Ballsacks, knowing I would do *anything* to make this right. From the moment I formulated my plan, widening my legs slightly and allowing them a better view of my arsehole, tilting my hips to enhance that view from their standing point. Parting my lips, moist from a slow lick of my tongue, whenever they showered me with their jizz.

I *made* them want me ... I made damn fucking sure of it.

For the first time in my life, I've used my body to gain advantage.

Fuck.

The thought settles deep within me, finding a comfortable place to sit amongst the shadows shading my insides. But it's not comfortable at all, it's the opposite.

For the first time in my life, I deserve my brand.

For the first time in my life, I'm every bit one of the whores they make us out to be. Only a far more sinister version, because I've got nothing left to lose ... but *everything* to gain.

A tear slides down my face as I take the cock of the man who spent the past twenty years emotionally abusing me, controlling me, fucking me, and slowly yet surely *moulding me* into something even my nightmares are afraid of.

CHAPTER THREE

He finishes in record time, dries his cock with a freshly laundered cloth he pulls from his jacket pocket, then grabs my face, holding it in a tight grip. "If you're well enough to chew someone's cock off then you're well enough to be active again. Time to rise into the light." He lets go of my face and unlocks my door, signalling for me to follow.

We walk through the dark catchment room, me clothed in nothing but blood. I note the lingering scent of citrus and sage. A scent I recognise…

Fuck.

Aero. He's been in here, and not too long ago.

This could really throw a cock in the works…

Did Aero watch me chew that man's penis off? I fucking hope not, he'll be having nightmares for the rest of his immortal goddamn life.

It doesn't make sense that he would come to this cum smeared shit hole knowing there is nothing he can do for me … if he's been listening, he knows how well guarded I am.

And after what I just did, I doubt that's going to change any time soon.

Kroe leads me up the ladder and through the open trap door, along the hallway and up the set of stairs into his personal chambers.

There's no light coming through the windows, night time then. The only way I could track the days down there was by counting the late Ballsacks' sleep cycles. But they took turns, so it was hard to tell day from night.

Kroe gestures to the ornate door that leads to his bedroom. "After you, Cupcake."

I hate sharing his bed, but I suspected this would happen tonight.

Again, I banked on it.

After witnessing the carnage I just created with my cock biting teeth, Kroe will keep me close. He will also want to put me back in my place … with his penis.

It's a good thing—my plan wouldn't work otherwise.

It's a good thing, Dell.

I try to still my trembling hands.

Fuck.

I open the door to the opulent bedroom—not the sort of room you'd expect from a man like Kroe, being all white with plush soft furnishings and natural wooden accents.

A wave of nausea rolls over me again and I run through to the bathing chambers, making it just in time to dry retch into the toilet.

Kroe runs a bath behind me, stripping off his clothing as I cradle the bowl, trembling like a nympho at an orgy. "Get in here with me when you're done. I want your arsehole clean."

Fucking wanker. I retch again, this time bringing up a small amount of bright red blood.

Damn.

I sigh, wipe my mouth and pull the chain, flushing the contents away.

Kroe's waist deep in the large stone tub, stretching out as the steam coils his hair further. The blood from his hands has stained the water a soft blushing pink.

"Come, Cupcake." He motions for me to join him. I repress the urge to vomit again—he's sheathed himself into most of my orifices while in this tub.

Stepping into the water opposite him, I sink into the warmth, sending the water a deeper ruby tone as the blood from my skin mixes with that from his own.

We're both monsters—him and I, in our own ways.

He leans forward, muscles rolling as he grabs a bar of soap from the holder, before snatching at my wrist and lathering the slippery substance all over my arm. "You're filthy. Tell me, have you been fucking around while you've been galivanting about on your own? How many men have you opened these pretty thighs to?" He edges forward and pushes his hand between my thighs, parting them, exposing my comatose vagina to him.

She's silent as a fucking mouse and I just don't get it—she usually *preens* at moments like this, no matter how much I'm crying on the inside. Maybe she knows I'm using her right now, banking on her eager beaver ways. Cunning wench. Always going against my fucking grain.

I guess we're going in dry.

He pushes the douche he just procured from the side of the bath up my arse and pumps it. "None, sir," I reply, wincing. "Only the ones that forced their way in." My voice sounds gritty as I tense around the contraption.

He quirks a brow and slips it out of me. "Really? Pray, do elaborate ..."

Bingo.

I nudge my beast even though she's a cowering, trembling mess. If my vagina won't be there for me right now then I need the other, more ruthless side of me to take the reins and show the twat how it's done. We girls have to stick together.

She's not sure she wants to play a part in this though. Not with him, not even in light of the bigger picture. I grip her by the scruff of her neck and force the bitch to the surface, because fuck it, I *need* her right now.

A cool calm washes over my body and I crack my neck to the side, rolling my shoulders slightly as I shuffle my hips forward, parting my thighs further.

Kroe quirks a brow.

"They cornered me in the alley, five of them …" I say, in a sultry, suggestive voice that isn't my own. But my beast is owning it, playing the part seamlessly. Kroe's interest is piqued, the vein in his neck pulsing.

"Go on," he grinds out.

"The big one shoved me against the wall. He didn't get me warmed up before he pushed himself inside me, then he began to move, fucking me so hard that the bricks tore at my skin and I thought his cock would tear me in two."

He's practically salivating now, probably getting off on the fact that, for once, I appear willing.

I shuffle my hips a little closer, lick my lips and arch my neck to expose my throat to the man I hate with *almost* every fibre of my being.

Closing my eyes, I arch my back. "He groped me while the others pumped their cocks, watching him move inside me, my arse rolling with the force."

I peek through my lashes. He's stroking himself, getting ready to rein my beast himself.

"And then?"

I bring my hand around and rub at my dry fucking vagina. I'm not kidding, even in a goddamn bath it's as dry as a fucking desert in there, but my beast is putting on a good show.

"He forced me to the ground, and another one fucked my mouth, pouring his cum down my throat while I choked on his cock. But I wanted it Kroe ... I wanted them *all* to fuck me."

That does it for him. He's flipping me over with a single movement and sheathing himself inside me, fucking me so hard I slip and crack my elbow on the side of the bath, causing me to lose hold on my beast who swiftly cowers back into the corner, shaking like a wounded pussy cat.

Looks like I'm on my own. Her and my vagina can fuck off, I don't need them anyway.

Shit I'm dry. Not to mention that well of courage that no longer exists. Damnit. But I can't back out ... it's all or nothing.

I don't realise I'm crying until a tear slips between my lips and the taste of salt smacks my buds.

Pull it together Dell, this is not the time to lose your testicles.

He's thrusting into me so firmly I can barely catch a breath. Silent tears drift aimlessly down my cheeks.

What's happening to me?

He's been asleep for a while, arm draped over my body, hand shackling my wrist. We're naked, his immaculate physique next to mine which is trailed with scars, as though a toddler drew all over me with a blade.

Starlight's shafting in through the open balcony door, illuminating the steady stream of tears still lining my cheeks. I couldn't stop them after the bath. At some point he realised I was crying and got off on the fact.

Kroe shifts in his sleep, removing his hand from my arm and rolling onto his back. I let out a shuddering breath I hadn't realised I was repressing, finally free of his branding fingers.

I look across, towards the monster sleeping next to me, and freeze.

Standing in the doorway is a silhouette I recognise ... very fucking well.

'Aero ...'

Fists clenched, stance wide and enough malice in those dimly lit eyes to suggest he's wrangling his dark side for purchase. My heart shutters over a few beats, finally finding its rhythm again before I can stress too much that I'm having a fucking coronary.

My vagina's doing a little somersault and I breathe a soft sigh of relief that she didn't die of starvation. She's such a hussy, apparently only in it now for the big, juicy god cock. She's developed expensive taste over the past month.

I try not to cry out, try not to jump out of bed and run directly towards him like a flailing damsel. *'What are you doing here?'* I yell in my head. I know he can't harm Kroe—the wards would probably kill my Dawn God if he tried. He has no more wishes to take from me either ... is he here to fucking *rescue me?*

He nods, taking a quiet step forward as he brings his finger to his lips, motioning for me to 'shhh'.

Yeah, ok, so I'm silently ugly crying. Big fucking deal.

Actually, it is. I never usually cry, but I'm just so bloody glad to see him that my sad tears have now turned to happy tears. Aero's here, for me ... walking towards me ... about to grab me and take me somewhere safe ...

He's four steps away. I can see his features so clearly now; eyes of molten amber surveying me all over for the damage I can see him scenting. But he's holding his feral side at bay ... maybe he's been practising.

Nope, I was wrong. His eyes are all black now—he's growling from his chest like a fucking animal.

Kroe shifts in his sleep. Aero freezes.

My gaze slides to Kroe as he brings his arm lazily back over my body, clamping his hand around my wrist and muttering something unintelligible.

I look back at Aero.

Fuck.

I was so excited to see him, so caught up in the moment that I almost lost sight of my fucking *game plan*, and I'm angry at myself.

I need to be so much better than this.

'There's something I need to do first, Aero,' I convey, and he shakes his head, taking another step towards me.

'You can't take me right now! He'll wake up and you'll get in trouble with the real motherfucking monster out there, probably even die.'

He shakes his head again, harder, baring those canines in their full, feral glory.

Stubborn fucking Fae God.

'I have to do this, you have to let me do this. Please! I won't be able to live with myself otherwise ...'

He hisses loudly, causing Kroe to stir and mumble. Another figure, all dark and broad shoulders, slips through the door and drags Aero out backwards, into the night.

Tears slide down my cheeks.

He cares ... is it too much to hope they all do? I know that's a bit fucking greedy of me, but I'm a little euphoric right now because Aero actually *cares*. And I'm in the good graces with my vagina again, which is a big bonus. That bitch has some serious fortitude, because I'm dubious of her ability to stretch enough to accommodate his god cock.

Anyway.

I'm rambling, because I know I just fucked off my Dawn God; because I know he's likely been listening to my internal jumble this entire time ... and he probably knows my plan. They *all* probably do.

He still tried to extract me, cheeky bastard.

He knew what he was doing, knew this plan of mine will likely cost me my life. Knew I'd willingly go with him if he showed up in my hour of need. Not that I blame him, I would've done anything in the world to save my mother, if I were able.

I want to tell Aero to trust me. I don't do it though, because I barely trust myself. Because I'm powerless, weak, useless and caged ... but beneath my skin lies someone else entirely; perhaps no more than a shadow, yes, but she's out to redeem herself to this world she failed a very long time ago.

CHAPTER FOUR

"Fuck, I've missed you." Kroe slips out of me and wipes himself clean of our residue.

My own shame oozes onto the sheets and I suppress the urge to groan, instead rolling over and pressing my face into the pillow, ignoring the fact that it smells heavily of Kroe. I really just want to go back to sleep, but a sharp slap to my bum fucks that dream right up the proverbial arsehole.

"Go get ready." He gestures towards me. "Powder that face up, some khol around your eyes, too. You look a fucking wreck. Can't be charging triple for a go at you if you look like that."

Nice one. Good thing I have thick skin. Who needs an ego anyway?

I hobble to the bathroom, hands between my legs, cupped to prevent any spillage staining the carpet. I reach the stone floor of the bathroom and begin to close the heavy wooden door.

"Leave that open. I need to see you at all times."

Bastard. I can't even pee in peace.

Pushing the door back open, I sigh, wrapping my arms

around my body. I'm not sure what it is about Kroe, but he makes me feel so fucking exposed.

I glance in the mirror, the one hanging over the excessively ornate wooden vanity, noting my swollen, puffy lids and bloodshot eyes. He wasn't lying. It's pretty obvious I've been crying most of the night. This is going to do terrible things for my reputation.

I haul out the glass box from beneath the vanity, where Kroe keeps a set of cosmetics for me, and try to patch the shit show that is my face.

When I walk back into the bedroom, war paint in place and my hair secured high, there's a skimpy red corset and something that barely qualifies as a skirt laid out on my pillow.

Kroe pushes back the covers and climbs out of bed, smoothing his hair back from his face. "Get dressed, the girls have been at it for an hour already. Don't want them thinking you get special treatment." He slaps my arse again then parades himself to the bathroom, where he proceeds to pee in my direct line of sight.

I finger the clothing and try not to heave my guts all over it. Special treatment? Fucking hell.

"Oh, and Cupcake? Oil your holes. It's going to be a long day." He throws me a wink as he shakes his penis off. Wanker.

I'm not oiling my fucking arsehole, because fuck him. That's why.

When we're both dressed Kroe gives me a scan over, squeezing my breasts and arse like he's testing to see whether I've been adequately baked. "You'll pass. Let's go."

He grabs my wrist and leads me out the door, into the hallway which curves around, then connects with the grand stone staircase in the centre of the building.

I take the moment to study the man who owns me—

tailored suit and hair slicked back, so shiny it gleams in the rich candlelight illuminating the halls. In an alternate universe, I'd find the fucker appealing. I wonder if it's a situation of circumstance that led him to be this way—though perhaps that's the insane part of me talking. The part that doesn't want him to die.

We pass a whore I know well—Muriel. We've often kept each other warm at night. Mousy coloured hair pinned high, boobs pushed to her chin and face painted thickly, she leads a middle-aged man with a face like a fish. He's dressed in finery that suggests he's a high payer, and therefore qualifies the use of one of the rooms upstairs.

My interest is drawn to her left hand, the curl of it unnatural against the soft fall of her skirt. I draw in a sharp breath, feel the blood drain from my face when I realise ... Muriel's hand is missing three fingers and a thumb.

Muriel never steps a foot out of line ... has *never* done anything to warrant even a slap on the wrist.

Fuck.

I lift my gaze to her face, seeking to understand. She's scowling at me, her upper lip curling back as her gaze drags over my body, before she leads fish face around the bend and disappears out of sight.

What the fuck was that? Surely that wasn't one of my girls hating on me?

I vomit into my throat then swallow it, the coppery tang of blood lingering as Kroe leads me down the grand, stone staircase.

The hall opens up before us—prevailing black undertones, rock surfaces wet with liquor and laden ash trays, ornate chandeliers, and lush velvet seaters caped in blood red. The scene is muted by a wispy film of smoke that smells both sweet and herbal. I have no idea what it's called, but the men smoke a lot of it. Unfortunately, the ones who smell the strongest of it can go for hours. Either that, or they struggle to get it up.

Other whores watch me keenly from where they are either serving drinks or men's penises, as Kroe leads me to a space in the crowd. Hundreds of men toil about, dragging their eyes over my scarcely clad body, licking their lips and whispering to each other.

Well, fuck. Quite a turn out. I don't think I've ever seen the place so full.

Kroe tucks me in close, his lips grazing my ear. "Wait here, I'll be right back." He pats me on the arse, before disappearing into the crowd.

Nobody approaches me. It's like I have some sort of invisible barrier around me, though almost everyone is watching me.

The men.

The women.

I wring my fingers together, strangling them as tension thrums through my muscles, a thick pulse of anxiety threatening to choke me.

Something doesn't feel right.

The place has been changed around. There's a new clearing in the middle of the main zone housing two fucking poles which look like giant erect cocks, replicas of the ones on the whipping dais.

Great … a fantasy stage for anyone who watched my public whipping pre-penis eating days.

Fuck me, it's going to be a long day.

A woman I recognise heads in the direction of the bar. There's a patch covering her left eye … the residue of a scar mottling the upper arch of her cheekbone, neither of which I remember her having.

Her expression is blank, empty … her hand is not.

She slides into me tightly, the action likely looking like an embrace between two fellow cum dumpsters.

"For Delta," she mumbles, running something sharp along the exposed skin between my corset and skirt. She drags it along my abdomen, parallel to my fucking scar and I suck a sharp breath through my teeth. She pushes away, a smirk curling her lips, then turns and disappears into the crowd.

What the fuck just happened?

Fighting to remain composed, I shift my body inconspicuously, feeling the cut with the tips of my fingers. It's shallow, more of a deep graze. Not done to maim … but a message. One received loud and fucking clear.

She's telling me I deserve everything I get.

I glance around the room as Kroe breaks through the crowd and strides back over to where I'm standing. "All for you, Cupcake," he purrs, gesturing about the room. "Your impending return has been quite the draw card over the past two weeks. The girls have done extra hours to keep up. Well … the ones who are still able."

His words twist at my insides as I absorb their meaning—panning my vision, forcing myself to take in details amongst the crowd.

Ariana, missing an arm. She used to help the girls apply makeup in the mornings. Malorie—she no longer has ears and her beautiful golden locks are gone; her shaved head mottled with red scars. Tanya, her gorgeous plump lips pulled tight in a sneer revealing fat, pink gums, without her trademark pearly white, straight teeth.

And there's Delta, swaying in a motherfucking sex swing over there. But not the Delta I know … not the Delta who's long, shapely legs were the envy of many, despite the extra unwanted attention they garnered. In their place are now angry, red stumps, rising and falling to the beat of the old man pumping away between them. She flicks me the bird and I almost fucking faint.

The women I don't recognise are fresh faced, new … most of them sans the womanly curves that signify the rise to womanhood.

Fucking hell.

My knees buckle and Kroe grabs me by the arm, pulling me against him. "Hold it together, Cupcake," he drawls, probably assuming I'm afraid of the stage he's set for me.

I'm not going to lie, that does look intimidating, but I'm a tough bitch and I know I can manage myself up there.

What I'm afraid of is the way my girls are sizing me up, looking at me like I'm one of the many men in this room about to take advantage of them for the price of a token.

They hold me accountable …

This is going to be much harder than I thought.

Kroe leads me towards the penis poles in the centre of the room, and my gaze falls on a swath of golden skin as we come to a halt at their base. My breath catches.

There, sitting on a stool in the corner of the bar, a large hat covering his golden curls but otherwise dressed similar to the fucktards patronising this event, is Drake. He's even wearing a red sash, the sight of which makes me want to vomit again. Apparently he's doing his best to blend in with the crowd.

His golden gaze holds me hostage and there's a subtle shake of his head.

What did he think I was going to do, yell to the crowd that the God of fucking Dusk is here in this brothel?

I avert my gaze before my rogue vaginal juices send all the men in this room ravenous, because he was looking at me in a way that made my heart ache—literally fucking ache, which was like a little flush button for my vagina. I press my hand to my chest to try and hold her together, because she's struggling along right now, probably because I've spent my whole life starved of affection and I just felt a whole wave of it in that one look. My heart gobbled it up, throwing me completely, which is not ideal because I've got a motherfucking job to do.

Drake cares, and he's about to see me get fucked a hundred ways to Sunday by most of the men in this room, and not be able to do a thing about it. Not an ideal situation when your Dusk God feeds off control.

We might end up with a rogue player on the board, and I don't want my Drake to become a victim of those wards …

Fuck.

Something cold clamps over my wrist and I look down.

What the fuck?

Kroe's smiling to himself like the cat who got the cum, though the girl standing next to him, Leila, is not smiling at all. She's scowling at me, her dirty blonde hair dishevelled, as if she put it up with fumbling hands rather than with the confident, deft movements I've witnessed when she works her hair into a style suitable for a day's worth of fuckery.

I follow her haunted gaze down, down, to where two tapered, bright red stumps hang limply before her.

Gone.

I stare, sick to my stomach yet mesmerised, blinking at those stumps … before finally shifting my gaze back to her eyes, hooded and dark, draped with bags that she's tried to cover with too much powder. Or perhaps it's just hard to apply when you have no hands.

"This, Cupcake," Kroe motions to the iron cuff around my wrist and the chain that flows to the sister cuff he's now placing around Leila's ankle, "is because I can't keep tabs on you *all* the time. I'd hate to lose my biggest asset again. So, Leila is your new buddy. You're not to communicate with her or I'll also take the hands of Kit, her sister over there."

I look to where he's pointing; to a small blonde girl who looks to be around fourteen, serving drinks behind the bar.

What bust she has is pressed high by the tight-fitting corset she wears, but at least she's behind the fucking bar that holds the rogue penises at bay.

Bar maids are strictly off limits, someone's got to be able to water the men. Hard to do with a cock in your arse.

Kroe's put Kit behind the bar as assurance that Leila won't talk to me or help me escape. Tactical arsehole. I want to scream because my plan is quickly going penis shaped.

I don't know if I can do what I need to do with my gods watching on, and I can't convince one of my girls to help me with my plan if they all hate me. Especially not if I have one so tightly bound to Kroe's whims, with a sister on the line if she doesn't oblige, chained to my fucking body.

Fuck.

I'm not going to get many chances at this—I'm going to have to take one when it comes and who bloody knows when that's going to be.

But I have to make this right, because I did this to my girls. Me.

I'm responsible for every limb lost, every finger, every slice of dignity or hope that's been shed from their already wounded bodies and souls.

It's with that thought that my arms are hoisted between the poles and, to cheers from the crowd, my clothes torn from my body and dropped, landing in a ruby swirl, reminiscent of a puddle of blood at my feet. Even my goddamn panties go, and I steal a glance at Drake...

He's staring at my scar, and probably the new graze above it, his face draining of all its glorious, godly colour.

Kroe stalks across the dais and back again, addressing the crowd in a booming voice. "Here is the fantasy I've promised you all. Finally, her back has healed enough, but not so much that you can't relish in the memory of the whips that were dragged across her skin for speaking out of turn."

I scan the circle of penises standing to attention, pressing against trouser linen left, right, and centre.

"She's triple the price of the regular but more than triple the pleasure. Who'll be the first to put this whore back in her place? She'll be here till nine lads, so you'll all get your chance! First in though, the tighter the grip on your cock."

Guess I should've been practising my pelvic floor exercises rather than spending my time luring Ballsacks for penis amputation purposes.

I dare to glance at Drake—note his knuckles, white around his glass, canines lengthening. To anyone else he would appear eager to go balls deep and put me in my place.

I see that he cares.

Leila sits next to the pole on my left. I search her eyes for a sign of comradeship but receive a seething glare in return. Trembling, I stare ahead. There's nothing more soul destroying than being isolated by your fellow cum dumpsters.

Drake can't see me like this. I thought I could handle myself but right now, under these circumstances, I'm not sure I can.

My beast is nowhere to be seen, I guess she doesn't want him to see her vulnerable side either.

I scream internally. 'Aero, unless he's just here to enjoy the fucking show, I need you to get Drake out of here. Please, there's nothing he can do anyway!'

No sign of him, only the crowd leering and chanting with their mugs held high, converging further to garner a closer view. Some old coot with white hair and a cruel smile pays a premium to have the first go at my twat that's still raw from Kroe's recent assaults.

'Please!' Still no fucking sign.

Drake moves to stand at the back of the crowd, towering over them all, watching from a distance as the old bastard approaches me. A warm wash trickles across my skin, as though I'm being wrapped in a blanket of pleasure that's caressing all my sensitive bits. Even my rogue vagina perks her ears up … sniffing at the air like she can sense one of her godly penises near-by.

I moan with delight, but it's incomplete, empty, because I know it's my Dusk God trying to make things better for me—doing everything in his power to make this fucked up situation *easier*.

Even so, I almost start dry humping the air in a desperate plea to gain some friction for my perked little flowerpot. I'm panicking, eyes darting around, a sheen of sweat covering my skin. 'AERO!'

Fucking hell. I can't do this …

I see a new movement in the crowd—a brush of black hair and olive skin half covered by a cap, just as the white-haired, premium paying fucker reaches my back.

Kal, please be Kal.

Please.

A flash of royal blue eyes, a glimpse of familiar lips, luscious and full …

Thank fuck.

Aero sent Kal … probably because Kal can calm Drake with his emotion controlling voodoo shit. He's a clever God, that one. A real forward thinker. When he's not all dark eyed and scary.

The man behind me takes his position, readying himself to spear me with his dick. My vagina's not even mad about it, because she's turned the fuck on thanks to Drake's administrations from afar.

The glass shatters in Drake's hand, sending dark liquid splattering all over himself. Those golden eyes relax then turn … *sultry*? His gaze shifts to Kal, who looks about ten shades of fucked off as he does everything to avoid looking in my direction.

Oh, I get it now … poor Kal. Forced to lure Drake out the only way he knows will work on our dusky horn dog …

Drake follows my Night God out of the room, chewing his own lip and pinching Kal's ripe arse on the way, earning him a feral hiss from Kal and a slap to the hand that *almost* makes me laugh, just before I'm pummelled by yet another unsanctioned penis, groaning in delight as my aching pleasure-puss finally gains some friction.

Seductive Kal, taking one for the team like a fucking boss. I just hope he's got the balls to back it up and keep Drake occupied all day.

Sorry, Kal. His arse looks strong enough to take the beating though.

I'm so fucking thankful, because this shit's mortifying enough as it is without having them watch on and spend the rest of their immortal years picturing me as a victim. No thank you.

But then the warmth subsides from my body—leaving me feeling, once again, cold and broken.

Drake's gone. It's bittersweet victory at its finest.

My vagina recedes within herself, disappearing into her clam shell. Bitch. The little tart couldn't find it in herself to stick around for the day, just to make things easier for me? I'll remember this next time she's pleading me for a petting.

This man is not being gentle. Not the best day to protest an oiling.

I try to dip myself into the blank space my mind goes whenever I have a strange man tossing himself off inside me, but I can't. I just can't fucking get there. Meaning I feel everything, both emotionally and physically as this group of men have their way with me; while Kroe benefits lucratively at my expense.

CHAPTER FIVE

Ten hours straight and I stopped counting the men who found their release inside me while the rest of them watched on.

Exhausted, chain dragging along the ground, I follow Leila up the stairs after our incredibly awkward bathing session—Leila glaring at me while she tried to wash her honey pot with two ineffective stumps. I wordlessly offered to help when I just couldn't take it any longer … if looks could kill.

Kroe had business to attend tonight, so Leila's on Dell patrol. Which means Kroe will be fanging for me by tomorrow night. Problem is, after today, I'm not sure how much more of this I can take.

At the top of the stairs we swing to the left, following a small trail of women, all fresh out of the bathing chambers too. Others follow behind and I can feel their eyes on the back of my head, their gazes scanning my half naked back that I couldn't clothe properly because of this stupid fucking chain. I'm going to freeze tonight. At least I'll have the girls to keep me warm, even if they aren't interested in exchanging pleasantries.

We make our way through a creaky door and down a familiar hallway that's dimly lit with rusty, sputtering old lanterns. Girls branch off through separate doors, some closing them behind them but some leaving them open, gaping at me and Leila as we pass.

We follow a busty redhead into the room at the end, one of the only dorms with a window; great in the summer, fucking torture in the winter when everyone does their best to avoid it.

The ground is cold beneath my feet and I look longingly towards the big bed pushed against the wall, with a single blanket that's been in this room since as long as I can remember. The lantern flickering in the corner highlights how weathered the mattress is, how stained the one pillow is, and how tired the other six girls appear to be.

One by one they climb onto the bed, curling themselves into each other and making room for the next, until Leila and I are the only two left standing.

She clambers onto the bed, her oversized shirt swimming about her body, and settles into the crook of another, snuggling in close as heavy pelts of rain lash the big bay window.

I follow, am halfway onto the bed when something, somebody, shoves against me, ramming me hard and fast in my stomach so that I land back on the ground with a thud.

Did one of my fellow whores just push me off the fucking bed?

Yes … that's exactly what happened, I realise, hauling myself into a sitting position and catching the heavy glares of seven women who look like they want to kill me in my sleep.

Well, fuck. Guess I'm keeping myself warm tonight.

A puff of air whistling through a small hole in the window snuffs out the lantern. We're plunged into darkness, apart from sporadic flashes of lightning slashing through the blackness.

I shuffle as far from the bed as I can manage in my manacled state, curling myself into a tight, quivering ball as bitter outside air torments my exposed skin.

My girls don't trust me anymore. Probably never will. How am I supposed to get them out of this fucking place if we can't work together?

They see the girl who got special treatment, then disappeared for an extended period of time with no heed for the well-being of her fellow whores.

Granted, I fucked up. I'll carry that burden for the rest of my life.

They don't see the girl who would put her life on the line for them. Who has, time and time again, not because I owe it to them, but because I *care* about them.

Because I *love* them.

For a long time, they were all that kept me alive.

I repress the sob that's threatening to expose my weaknesses to them, wishing my emotional sensory button wasn't malfunctioning. Or maybe it's actually *functioning* for a change…

The room slowly fills with heavy, sleep-laden breathing. I've always envied the other girls for their ability to sleep so well—exhausted from the day's fuckery. Even asleep, I dream of shit that throws me straight back into consciousness again, generally breathless and sweating like an overexcited twat.

I wish I was sweaty right now. Instead I'm fucking freezing, pushing big huffs of air at myself and jiggling against the hard, cold floor, trying to create friction. But it's useless… and I'm hurting—my poor vagina's throbbing, and not in the way which garners a night time fondle.

This is all for them… there's no point otherwise. But I

can practically feel the hate rolling off them in thick, poisonous waves.

I'm alone.

I gulp air, swallow the ache in my throat, blink back tears.

All I want is a cuddle.

All I want is my mother's arms wrapped around me, her breath on my face as she strokes at my hair, telling me it's going to be okay, even if it's a lie.

Another flash of lightning slices through the darkness and I'm suddenly wrapped in a pair of thick, strong arms—my body pressed firmly against the toasty warm one curled around me.

I become rigid. Gasping, I tug my head free from my Dell cocoon, drawing a deep lung-full of air and ... Kal's scent?

Kal.

I nuzzle my face into his chest, throat thickening, eyes stinging with unshed tears.

"I'm here. You're not alone ..."

My body heaves, the emotion spewing out of me as those walls come crashing down.

He's warm, his touch gentle as his hand makes small circular movements across my back, soothing my silent tears, pressing me closer into him, holding me tightly, protecting me against the sea of hatred threatening to drown my will.

He's here with me, comforting me, dealing with my backlash because I bound the Sun Gods to my fucking soul. I made him seduce Drake to distract the bastard ... he's probably copped just as much dick as I have today.

"I'm sorry ..." I whisper through a rogue hiccup.

Another bolt of lightning smacks the room into view, and I look up to catch a fleeting glimpse of Kal's troubled expression.

"Don't ever fucking apologise. Not to me, not ever," he whispers fiercely, his lips brushing my ear. There's an authority to his voice that I didn't expect to hear from Kal. "Do you understand? You apologise for *nothing*."

Well, fuck me. That just makes me cry harder.

He smooths the hair from my face, runs a thumb across my cheekbone then dips his face in closer, lips caressing my skin, kissing my tears with butterfly tenderness and catching them as they fall.

I revel in the way his stubble scrapes across my skin, agitating it enough to remind me that this is real. I'm stripped to the bones, splayed bare … but Kal's here. He cares.

His lips skim the corner of my mouth and he presses the gentlest kiss against the damp skin there. "It's going to be okay."

I draw his breath into my lungs, absorbing his words, letting them flood through me and warm me from the inside ….

It's not going to be okay though. He doesn't see it yet, but he will.

Still … he can't lie. The fact that he believes the words to be true gives me something almost tangible to cling to.

He loosens a deep breath and I allow him to tug me closer, though I'm careful to keep my iron shackle and chain from touching him. It's a bad case of irony that Kroe shackled me in the one weakness of any High Fae. I don't want to burn my Night God while he's fucking consoling me.

"Do you want me to help you sleep?"

I want to tell him no, I don't want that at all. I want this moment to last forever … so I don't have to face the bitter taste of reality.

Instead, I nod into his chest. I'm going to need my sleep if I want to survive long enough to make a difference.

He presses his lips against my mass of unruly curls, holding it for a good few seconds before I start to drift off, but not before I hear the muffled words Kal speaks into my hair. "You're ours. We're not letting you go."

Lights out.

I went to sleep with the God of Night wrapped around me and I woke up with Leila all up in my face. She sounds like a sweet little pixie that wants to chew my fucking head off, though miraculously, the rest of the girls behind her are still slumbering peacefully.

"Do you know how hard it is to give a man a hand-job with no fucking hands?" she whisper-yells, her face contorted with barely suppressed anger.

I hate thinking about penises this early in the morning, so I'm trying not to picture it while I rub at my sleep ridden face, tugging myself into a sitting position.

"Really fucking hard. You may be his '*Cupcake*', but you're dead to us, bitch."

Woah, fucking woah.

Dead?

This is worse than I thought, way worse than I could've imagined. Nobody else is going to have the guts to talk to me while Leila the Brave is chained to my traitorous body. It's now or never.

"Wait, please, I want to help." I reach for her but she rears back, causing me to tumble forward.

"Fuck off, slag," she hisses, and a couple of the girls stir. I blink wildly at Leila. Seems that word's contagious.

"I want to *help*!" I say it again, holding my hands up in submission.

She holds my gaze, unblinking, as though considering and then ... "I'm not sure what help you think your magic cunt can do for us anymore. I shouldn't even be talking to you!"

Magic cunt? That's a bit fucking dramatic. "Then why are you?"

She squares her slight shoulders, narrowing her eyes and peering down her nose at me. "Because you took the whipping for Lucy."

Right. Of course. "Did … did she survive?"

"No."

Fuck it. The lump that forms in my throat threatens to choke me. Don't ask questions you aren't prepared to hear the answers to, I guess.

"I'm sorry …"

"No," she says, shaking her head. "I'm done. You taking that whipping, it doesn't even begin to make up for the shit we went through while you were away."

"I didn't say it does … I'm just asking for a chance here, Leila."

"Stop," she says, shaking her head, lifting her stump to my face as if to shush me with an absent hand. "We're done with you, okay? All of us." She turns to drag me towards the door, probably to the bathing chamber so she can relieve herself while I stand on awkwardly and try not to listen. It's as uncomfortable as it sounds, even for a couple of girls who have no dignity left.

Time to go balls deep.

"There's an escape route in the downstairs bathroom," I blurt out, my words sounding loud and hollow in the cold room.

She spins to look at me, eyes wide as saucers. "What?"

If she hands my rebellious arse in, I'm dead. But I'm too far gone now.

"I have access to herbs to dose the drinks of the guards. If Kroe decides he wants a taste of his 'Cupcake' tonight, I'll make sure he's distracted for long enough past mid moon for you to get everyone out. There will be camels waiting under the old bridge on the outskirts of Hind Meadow. They'll be saddled with enough supplies to get you and the girls across the desert to the East."

I still need to confirm that with Aero. Not now though ... no point in having a bunch of camels sitting there for days on end drawing suspicion, getting tired, cranky, and spitting on each other if nobody's going to fucking need them.

She cocks her head to the side, studying me anew, perhaps weighing my worth. Finally, she drops her gaze to her stubs. "Why are you doing this? You left us to rot. You were free. Why, Dell?"

I suck in a sharp breath. Good fucking question, one that has many answers, but only one broad enough for her to really understand.

I wait for her to look up before I answer, so she can see the sincerity in my eyes. "Because I forgot who I was. I'll never forget again."

She frowns. "How do I know you're not just weeding out the rebels for Kroe?"

"You don't." I reach out and touch her arm. "Trust me, please."

She shakes her head, though she looks tentative in the motion.

Fucking hell. Guess I'm pulling out all my cards this morning.

"This scar?" I point to the one that drags down my forearm—thick, ugly and raised. "It's from the time Kaya took an extra loaf of bread from the kitchen. Kroe noticed, was bleating about taking some hands, so I took the fall."

Her eyes roam the scar, brow creased, before they travel down to a large patch of burnt flesh on my upper thigh.

"That one," I pull the chain back and shift my leg

slightly, to garner us a better view of the carnage in the low light. "He poured a kettle of boiling water on my thigh when he realised I was slipping my rations into a handkerchief, then giving them to Delta. She was being starved out for crying during sex when she had a urinary tract infection."

She nods, studying the damage intently. "I remember." She lifts her eyes to the scar peeping out on my clavicle.

I tug my top further across, revealing the fact that it runs all the way along it, then dips between my breasts.

"What about that one?"

Peering down, I clear my throat as I run my fingers along the smooth, silver scar. "That one ... you fell asleep on the job, early in the day when people tend to notice that shit. I think you had the flu at the time."

"I remember that day ..."

I nod.

"I noticed Kroe coming over to investigate, so I started yelling profanities at the top of my lungs. It woke you up, distracted Kroe, and he almost sliced my tit off for it."

She sucks a sharp breath through her teeth, and I inwardly chastise myself for not folding the truth. "Dell ..."

I shake my head. "I don't want your sympathy, Leila. I just want your help. We have a chance to get these girls out, one fucking chance. Are you with me, or are we going to sit by while everyone fucking dies here?"

She watches me with wide eyes and a broken expression. A heavy moment passes, my body trembling with anticipation. "Okay," she finally whispers, nodding slightly, then more eagerly.

"Ok?" I whisper back, and she nods again. Then we're both nodding together like a little rebellious cheer squad. Go team.

"I need a knife, and I need you to escort me down to the

storage room," I instruct, and she looks at me like I'm mad. She's not too far off the mark.

"How do you expect me to get you a knife? I'm chained to your fucking wrist, remember?"

I look down at her ankle. Yeah, a bit inconvenient that.

"What about Tammy? She works in the kitchen and also cleans Kroe's room. Is she …?"

With no hesitation, Leila nods. "You … *we* can trust her."

"Would you be able to get a note to her to slip a knife under the left side of his mattress before tonight?"

I don't think I could do it without a knife, it would become too personal if I had to strangle the bastard. My beast is fucking cowering at *that* idea, fur all pale and sickly looking.

Finally, she nods. "I think so. I'll do my best, though Tammy only has one foot now."

I suck in a breath, the weight on my shoulders compounding. Fuck, that's one very good reason for her *not* to trust me.

Leila shakes her head. "She got gangrene after she dropped a knife through her foot. Never play footsies with a man's balls if you have an open wound there."

"Oh." Crisis averted. "Can she make it up the stairs still?"

Leila nods. "She gets around."

Don't we all.

"Good. She'll also need to slip you a couple of butter knives. You'll need them to wedge up the trap door in the bathroom, in case it's fused from lack of use."

"Do you want a hand with anything else?" She waves her stubs at me.

I think she's having a joke but I repress the urge to smile, because that would be fucking inappropriate of me considering she wanted to cut me a new arsehole only five minutes ago.

I shake my head. "That's it. Just get as many out as you can."

I'm aware that some of the girls will choose to stay behind for fear of losing their heads, and others will be too sick, weak, or disabled to make the trip.

"I'll show you the way out once we reach the storage room."

She narrows her hazel eyes at me. "The dusty fucking storage room? Really?"

"Yeah." I sigh, remembering the carnage the girls are likely going to walk into if Kroe hasn't cleaned it up yet. "It's more than just a storage room."

Much more than just a fucking storage room.

During our bathroom break, I quietly point out the hatch to Leila and she whispers to one of the kitchen girls who's in the bathing chambers at the same time as us. Lucky fucking timing right there.

We must look like a couple of misfits; Leila in an oversized shirt with no pants or underwear, me still wearing the top that's only half covering my upper body, and not in the cute crop top kind of way. It's awkward ... fucking chains.

I lead her back up the stairs, looking both ways before we swing right at the top of the staircase. I really hope Kroe didn't come home early last night ... that would throw a penis in our plan.

Kroe's door is large and really fucking heavy. It creaks and groans as I tentatively open it enough for two skinny whores to pass through. I drag Leila into the sitting room after me, and push the bastard shut again.

The door to Kroe's bedroom is closed ... but that's not indicative of anything. He could be there; he could be out still. I'm counting on the fact that, either way, he usually sleeps later than this. Usually.

I bring my finger to my lips and Leila nods, though she looks more inclined to vomit than she does to speak. Being careful not to rattle the chains, we cross the room to the door on the far wall. I open the fucker and drag Leila through, shutting it after us.

"Fucking hell..." she gasps.

"Not far from the truth," I murmur, taking her stub in my hand and leading her down the dark and dusty staircase to the landing where I push the door to the storage room open, revealing the dusty world beyond, and sneeze.

Motherfucker. This allergy really is a pain in the arse.

We make it three steps in, Leila eyeing me like I'm about to detonate as I fan my face sporadically, before I sneeze again.

I swear it's gotten dustier in here.

"Can't you just stick some fucking cloth up that thing and block it up? Someone's going to hear us."

I wipe my nose cum on my low-slung sleeping pants. "Sorry."

Luckily, it's still early—too early for anybody to be down here. Even so, I quickly lead Leila through the obstacles, helping her when needed. After a few minutes we reach my grate and I give one of the metal bars a jiggle to shift it from its confines. Turning, I wave the bar at Leila.

She gapes at me like she's preparing to deep throat a chode. "How the *fuck?*"

Shrugging, I place the bar back in the grate. "I wore several butter knives down to the nub doing that. It took me four years and half my fucking sanity, but it was worth it in the end."

"I ... don't know what to say to that."

"Come on." I drag Leila by her non-hand back through

the obstacles—the chain in my other hand, trying to stop it from jingling like a sleigh ride.

I lift the lid to the blanket box and pull out my trusty dusty lantern, flicking it on, at the same time almost sneezing my brain out through my nose holes.

Lantern lighting our way, I lead Leila back into the hall and over to the trap door, where I kneel and work to wrangle the heavy bitch open.

The stench of death that wafts out as the seal breaks is thick, my beast now watching with piqued interest. She wants to catch a glimpse of her handy work, fucking savage.

Even through the stench, I can still smell those seven years I spent down there.

"Hold your breath and try not to scream." I settle the trap door open and make my way down the ladder one handed, with my oil lamp in the other, hoping the chain isn't going to make too much noise as we drag it down the rungs.

I make it to the bottom and quickly pan my vision. The door to my 'home' is wide open, revealing the carnage still inside.

The sight, the smell, and the memory are all too much. My guts explode through my nose and mouth, splattering across the floor in a bright red gush.

"Fuck, Dell … are you ok?"

Glancing sideways at Leila, I wipe my mouth and straighten.

"Fine."

"Dell … that's blood."

"I said I'm fine."

"Sure. Whatever you say." She draws a deep breath through her nose, brow furrowing. "It smells like *you* in there, Dell. Why the fuck does it smell like you in there?"

I shrug. "Don't think on it, it's just a fucking room, okay? I told you to block your motherfucking nose."

"It's hard to block my nose without fingers, you knob!"

"You're a smart girl, you know what I mean! From the inside."

"Smart enough to get teamed up with the girl with a fucking death wish and skin made of steel. How did you not cry during that whipping? It looked like it almost killed you."

"I'm broken. Now block your nose." She rolls her eyes.

"Ok, done." Her voice sounds all nasally.

Good. Time to get this over with.

I unleash my beast and she rears her pretty little head, salivating over the scent of her inflicted carnage through the door. Yeah ... she can deal with this.

Hips swaying, we lead Leila through the door. It's her turn to gag as we step over the two bloated bodies on the floor.

She points to the severed cock. "Is that what I think it is?"

My beast licks her chops like the animal she is.

"You've seen enough of them in your life to know that's a fucking penis without asking me, Leila."

She goes bone fucking white. "How the hell did his penis end up severed from his fucking body?"

My beast kneels on a clean patch of floor and we shuffle beneath the bed, fingering the edges of my blood painted love heart rock and prying it out of place. We fish around the hole for the small satchel of dried herbs Marion gave me, around the same time she gave me herbs to ward off the night sickness. These herbs, however, warded off another type of sickness—the sickness of the mind, by allowing me to have long rested sleeps.

My beast replaces the rock. We wriggle out from beneath the bed, and stand. Leila's staring at the severed penis, lying like a one-eyed snake, dead on the ground.

I shrug a shoulder. Well, my beast does. She's purring,

admiring her fucking handiwork. "He put his cock down my throat and I bit it off."

"You bit his fucking cock off?"

My beast gives the flaccid, shrivelled organ a nudge with my bare foot. It makes a flopping sound as it rolls over. "It would appear so."

Looking up at the ceiling, we point at the trap door above. "Through there, into here, out the door, up the fucking ladder, into the storage room and off to fucking freedom. Stick to the shadows, travel in small groups. Assign leaders and followers. Got it?"

Leila nods, though she's looking at me like she doesn't know me.

Wrangling my beast slightly so I have a chance to get a word in, I walk to Leila, taking her shoulders in my hands. "This carnage is my doing, but it's not who I am. It's who I've become to survive. It's who I need to be to save us."

Our eyes lock and in hers I see confusion, fear and longing. Longing to be free? Finally, she drops her gaze. "What's in the bag?".

"Dogwood. Ground up. Good shit. I only needed a little and it would knock me out cold. It got me through … never mind. We need to get it into the guard's drinks tonight."

Leila chews her lip as though considering, and then looks at me, eyes bright. "Kit's on the bar again. She'd do it, I know she would."

"Are you sure, Leila?"

"Don't worry, she can be trusted. Fuck knows she doesn't want to lose her hands too, but if there's a half sure way out of here, she'll give it a go."

We nod; my beast approves of this girl. I let said beast survey the carnage once more; she's so damn proud of her work, before we sashay out of the room like we fucking own the show.

It's only once we get back to the downstairs bathroom to wash and apply our makeup for the day that I rein my beast all the way in, and barely make it to the toilet in time to vomit up another wad of blood.

Fuck you, body. Pull it together. We have a job to do.

CHAPTER SIX

I tuck the satchel of Dogwood down the front of my corset, along with a note Leila scribbled on a piece of parchment with a sliver of coal poised between her stumps, part of her own secret stash she had tucked away inside a mattress.

We make our way to the main sex hall and walk to the bar, where Kit is on duty again. With a slight nod to her I slip the satchel out from between my bulging boobs, then discreetly tuck it behind the bar, at the same time asking for a glass of water each for myself and Leila.

Tonight, when the customers have left, and after a signal from Leila, Kit will spike the guards' after-hours drinks with enough dogwood that they each fall into a long, deep sleep.

With a knowing nod, Kit hands our drinks over, a 'special' water loaded with a concoction of vitamins that give us the energy required to last a day of fuckery. Kroe hates us going to work on a full stomach, doesn't want us vomiting all over the customers during sex, so this was his way around *that* little hurdle.

After so many years my internal digestive system has

gotten used to only expecting one meal a day, but I look forward to it because it's always hot and relatively nourishing. The one pro of being a hoe.

We finish our water then make our way into position, along with all the other girls who've filed into the room, faces cleverly painted to make them appear rested.

"There she is …" Kroe's voice booms down the stairs and I turn to see him reach the landing, then make a beeline for me and Leila standing by the 'stage'.

He gets right up in my face, slipping his hand beneath my skimpy skirt and wrapping his palm around my right arse cheek. "I missed you last night, Cupcake. I had my cock plunged into this randy little hoe, but she just wasn't as tight as you, you know? We have a thing, you and I." He pinches my chin, tilting my head up so we're matched, eye to eye as he kneads my arse. "I can't wait to watch the men fuck you today. I love watching the cum dribble down your legs while you take cock after cock, trying to hide the fact that you fucking love it."

The clock strikes ten and I fight the urge to vomit again. Hold it together body, you're better than this.

The guards throw the front doors open and a herd of men flood the room, smoking cigars and prancing about like peacocks as they find somewhere to sit, observe, or fuck. Hunting their own targets in the crowd of red-skirted women.

"You're mine tonight, Cupcake. Enjoy the foreplay." Kroe saunters off into the crowd like he fucking owns the joint, which he does.

Leila gives me a hopeful, knowing look, and I allow a small smile in return, trying to appear brave, even though my insides are churning.

It doesn't help that my vagina's still missing in action, only showing up for one of my Gods. Not that I want them here right now, I don't, because I can already tell today's going to be savage. The men have a ravenous gleam in their eyes as my hands are again tied to the two giant schlong poles.

I consider letting my beast free for the day, letting *her* deal with it all ... but no. I'm afraid she'll chew someone else's penis off and ruin the whole thing. Her ears perk up at the thought and she licks her chops. Savage bitch.

A swathe of white hair catches my eye as the clothing is pulled from my body. My heart does a little leap. Sol?

A tang of unsanctioned disappointment surges through me as I scan the swarming, drooling crowd, while someone lines themselves up behind me, right at my arsehole.

No, no ... he's not here. That's a good thing, Dell.

It's a good thing.

At some point I must have passed out hanging between these two erect schlongs. I'm not sure how long I've been out for, but when I come to, it's dark outside ...

Fuck.

I was going to wait until dusk to organise the camels, in case things went penis shaped during the day ... fucking missed that boat didn't I.

'Aero, I need your help,' I internally yell to my Dawn God who I hope is paying attention. Probably not, because he's a super important God. 'Please, *please* be listening. I need twenty camels fully loaded with enough food and water to make it across the desert, carrying a bunch of clothing that's not fucking red, waiting under the old bridge at the back end of Hind Meadow. Tonight. I know it's a lot to ask, but please. I'm *begging you.*'

Hoping he's busy hoarding and organising a bunch of

spitting camels for me, I wink at Leila. She's lying on the ground beside me, on top of one man with another plunging her pucker. She's not even bothering to pretend like she's enjoying it; these men are too drunk and savage now to notice the difference anyway. It's witching hour at the brothel, near closing time when all the men start to spit the dummy and let their inner demons come out for a final fuck.

Wincing, she gives Kit a slight nod; the signal.

Good, fucking swell, though I barely have the energy to be happy because I think my vagina has finally drowned in seminal fluid. I'm going to have a little funeral for her later, once I'm not so goddamn anxious. Maybe even try to revive her.

A man pays Kroe extra to have his cock in me while Leila works the stub of her thin arm up his arsehole, which he appears to thoroughly enjoy. I imagine Leila enjoys it too, plunging one of *them* for once rather than receiving the treatment herself.

When he's finally done with his fantasy, Kroe saunters over to our stage, looking immaculate in the new suit he probably splurged on from all the extra income he's been making over the past two weeks.

"That was fucking delightful, girls. I think I'll take you both with me to my room tonight, I have a few ideas I'd like to play around with."

I freeze, holding back the bile that's working its way up my throat.

Fuck.

I glance at the clock—nine fifty. The drinks for the guards are already lined up on the bar. I dare not risk a peak at Leila, I know she'll be freaking out as much as I am.

We told Kit to use all the fucking herbs, too. Just to be sure … and the camels are probably already there, spitting all over each other.

This is going to be all for nothing.

The room flashes bright.

Goddammit.

God fucking dammit.

Standing before Kroe, is Aero ... looking savage wearing a chest plate of bronze fucking god wear, like he's dressed for a bloody coronation or some shit, not a whore house.

What the fuck is he doing here?

My vagina does a little dance, and I rejoice in the fact that she didn't drown after all. But he's not looking at me with those hooded eyes ... which makes her pause her little mating dance. He's giving a *different* girl his fucking attention.

A hushed silence falls across the room and everyone kneels, except me, because I'm suspended between two giant wooden schlongs. Come to think of it, I've never knelt to them before ... they must think I'm super disrespectful. Should probably remedy that.

"To what do we owe the honour?" Kroe gushes, shuffling forward to kiss Aero's feet.

Aero accepts the grovelling, looking positively sinister as he does so, then swipes a dismissive hand at Kroe. "Enough. I'm here for cunt, not cock."

I cough. '*Say what now?*'

"Yes, Milord ..." Kroe slowly rises, motioning towards me. "I offer you the rebel here, strung between the poles. She's the one who spoke out of turn and was whipped for it. Perhaps substance to enliven your own fantasies?"

My vagina isn't sure what to do at the moment. She's half riding the edge of an orgasm at the prospect of having Aero's giant cock nestled inside her, brave twat, but half weirded the fuck out that he would take advantage of her in her current situation.

Aero throws Kroe a look of disgust, barely glancing my way. "I couldn't get off from *that* if I tried."

Wow. My vagina just fucking fainted, not to mention my achy-breaky heart.

Wait, I see what he did there ... 'couldn't get off from *that*'? He's probably referring to my dramatic staged event, which represents my torture. Not *me* in general. Well ... at least I hope that's what he's referring to.

"I want her." He gestures towards Leila. "They don't need hands for me to fuck them into a pulp."

Holy. Fucking. Hell.

Clever God. Taking Leila out of Kroe's equation for the night ... years of immortality hasn't *just* engorged the head on his penis, after all. Seems it's done some good for his brain as well.

"Yes, my Lord!" Kroe gushes. "Of course. I'll just unchain her from the slag, here." That fucking word again. The next person to use it is going to get ripped a new arsehole.

I roll my eyes, refusing to look at Aero, who's working around his restrictions to salvage the whole situation I've got going on here. It's kind of gallant, in a really fucked up way. Still, I'm pissed. He's about to fuck Leila into oblivion before he's even had the chance to fuck *me* into oblivion. I want to be the one to peel that bronze chest plate from his hard fucking chest!

Aero motions Leila towards that red velvet sex lounger over there, in my direct line of goddamn sight.

No ...

'Really?!' I think yell. 'You can't be fucking serious! Can't you get a room?'

I've been watching people bang on that thing all day, I never pictured my Dawn God would be using it to drape somebody over, and certainly not someone other than *me*.

Leila's watching me with wide, frightened eyes as one of

the younger girls wipes her down with a damp cloth, and the sex lounger is scrubbed clean for the big shiny God and his little toy whore.

Kroe rips the last shred of dignity from Leila's body—the scarce piece of lingerie that strategically covers her scar, if nothing else. Bastard. I worked so hard to pull that thing down over her shoulders, too.

Leila sheds a tear, entirely exposed.

"Now you can see *all* the damage, Milord."

Aero growls, deep in his chest. "Fuck off, I'm trying to enjoy my meal."

"Yes, Milord." Kroe drops faster than a pair of prostitute's panties, slithering back into the crowd like the serpent he is.

The rest of the men in the room have given Aero a wide berth, plenty of space for him to spread his wings if he wishes. I know from experience just how much High Fae like to show them off while they're fucking.

I'm swallowing bile that's smeared with a metallic sheen as another man lines up behind me, probably my last paying customer of the day. He grabs my hair, ripping my head so far to the side that I let out a strangled scream.

"I paid triple to make you bleed, filthy whore."

Aero's darkening gaze snaps to me, even as he tips Leila over the seater and starts unbuttoning his pants, canines lengthening.

He's angry at the fucker behind me, I can feel it, smell it, sense it rolling off him like a wave.

'Calm down.'

Leila may look frightened, but I can smell her desire … it's practically dripping off her. I don't blame her, not with the majestic God standing behind her, parting her legs and readying to plunge her nether regions.

Her mind is frightened, but her body thinks otherwise.

Aero's eyes reel me in as he slides his fingers through

Leila's folds, before freeing his large throbbing self and following the path his fingers just took with the head of his penis, paying special attention to her clit.

Leila's look of fear turns to one of surprise and then pleasure. She moans a little, and gently tilts her hips to gain him better access.

But Aero's not looking at her—he's looking at me. My vagina just roused from her dramatic exit.

The bastard behind me thrusts his cock into my arse at the same time Aero drives his impressive length into Leila's overstretched vagina, though she doesn't look pained about it. In fact, she brings one of her stubs down between her legs and shamelessly starts working herself from the front, her expression one of pure pleasure. She's rocking herself onto his shaft just as much as he's working her from behind.

Dickhead behind me, however, he's working me like he's plunging a pipe, though I suppose that's exactly what he's doing. His fist gripping my hair, keeping my neck arched and vulnerable, he fucks me so hard my wrists begin to bleed from the pressure applied to my bonds. I ignore the pain, instead focusing on Aero's cock sliding in and out of Leila's honey trench while she moans like we were all taught to, except I think hers are actually *genuine*.

I feel the moisture coating my vagina much quicker than the idiot behind me smells it. "You're fucking enjoying this, aren't you? You're not meant to like it! That's not what I paid for!" He tears at my nipple with his fingers, leaving a sharp burn in its wake.

Aero growls, low and deep, still holding my eye contact as I grit my teeth against the pain.

'Stop looking at me, people will notice.'

He shakes his fucking head. Disobedient Dawn God.

I hate that he's seeing me like this, even if my vagina's getting satisfaction from the way he's coaxing Leila towards climax. I feel like my wrists are about to break from the pressure, but my mind's so focused on Aero sliding in and out of her that the pain's just subdued background noise ... in and out, in and out.

Most of the crowd continue to bow to the gleaming God before them, fucking a whore in one of their brothels. They're probably going to go home thinking they're all blessed or some shit.

Aero bares his teeth and stops his rhythmic thrusting, his wings unfolding from his back, stretching to their full, glorious span to the gasps and murmurs of the crowd, a second before I feel the sharp sting of *teeth* sinking into my neck ...

What.

The

Fuck.

I scream. Nobody's ever *bitten* me before!

Aero's jaw is clenched, nostrils flared, muscles bulging as his wings break off the view of an entire portion of the crowd. Everyone else probably thinks their Dawn God is enjoying the show. Maybe he is, maybe I'm wrong about him. Maybe his wings came out because he was close to climax ... not because he's being a territorial bastard.

I scream again, eyes rolling back as the fucker sinks his teeth in further. My hands are cut from my bonds and the man is pried from my floppy body that's about as useful as a limp dick.

"You got your blood, time to fuck off." Kroe scoops me up and carries me away.

He smells like sardines again. I fucking hate sardines.

CHAPTER SEVEN

The resident healer tended my wounds, dousing me in herbs for pain relief, and also to stop the delirium—the weird semi-sexual fantasies I could barely make heads nor tails of. So fucking strange.

We're not meant to bite other people. We're taught to never use our mouths unless someone puts their cock in it, and even then, we have to be careful not to cut them. I guess that makes a hell of a lot more sense to me now …

While I was being tended, I asked for something to give me an energy boost, knowing I'll be needing it later tonight. She obliged and gave me a leaf to chew that left me feeling really fucking jacked.

Kroe collected me so I could bathe in his chambers, preferring me to use his personal soaps and lotions when he's intending to pound me for the night.

"You're looking as fresh as a daisy again. Did you do the douche?" Kroe hates mixing his own semen with that of other men.

I nod as I pad towards the bed, my hair still damp from the bath.

"Good, your arsehole, too?"

I nod again. Wanker—I know how to clean myself after a hard day of fuckery. They think we're all savage animals, what they *don't* realise is that women are much smarter than men, because our brain capacity isn't shared between two entirely separate heads.

Ok, that's sexist. And not true. But it sounds good.

"Come over here." He signals for me to join him on the massive bed he's splayed naked across, eating from a tray piled high with food.

Wincing, I shuffle towards the bed.

"You sore, Cupcake?"

Another nod as I gently lower myself onto the bed. Yes, I am sore, because my vagina's given up on me *again*, and right now I really fucking need her if I'm going to screw this man until he's so satiated that he passes out and falls into his deepest sleep ever.

"Lay down on your stomach and take some food from the plate. I'll smear some ointment on you."

Ointment sounds great, though I wish it was the sort Aero had; to numb my nether regions entirely. Especially if she's not going to rise to the occasion and give a girl a hand.

No answer from my vagina. Twat.

The food smells good, but even the sight of it is making my stomach churn.

Kroe lifts a brow at me as he pops a cherry tomato into his mouth. "Eat. You're starting to lose your curves we worked so hard to procure."

Fucker. I nibble at a piece of potato, hoping I keep it down.

He parts my legs, exposing me to him entirely and I battle my inner urge to wiggle away—that just wouldn't work for me right now. He expels a lot of energy when he's chasing me around the room. It's kind of like a fucked-up version of cat and mouse, and I need this man to trust me, to be well and truly sucked into an orgasm stupor if my plan's going to work at all.

"She did take a pounding today, didn't she?" He rubs his fingers along my folds, being uncharacteristically tender as he smears a gooey substance over me, *through* me ...

And my vagina just woke the fuck up, because he referred directly to *her*. She fucking loves that shit. Plus, it was *this* man who broke her in, who gave the bitch her first orgasm.

She hates him, but at the same time, she loves him, because she's a trillion levels of fucked up.

She dampens herself for him, picking up where Aero's display left her earlier.

Kroe sucks in a sharp breath. "She's missed me, hasn't she? She's so ready for me already ..."

Fuck my life. Fuck my vagina. Fuck everything.

I'm contradicting myself right now and I don't fucking care, because I'm experiencing some serious identity trauma. Do I give in and enjoy this man? It's what he wants, even if he is about a million levels of fucked up himself.

I look over to the clock on the mantle as my juices continue to flow ... two hours until midnight. Two hours to get this man well and truly fucked.

You can do this, Dell, even if you hate yourself for it for the rest of your very short life.

'Forgive me, Aero.' I wish he couldn't hear all this ...

I set the bitch loose, tilting my hips and exposing myself to him fully.

My vagina dribbles all over herself—she loves the fact that I'm playing along. But I'm not just playing along anymore ... I'm doing this just as much as she is. Because I hate this man, but I also fucking love him ...

"Fuck, Dell ... you've never been so ready for me before." He slips his fingers through my folds, paying special attention to my clit. My hips begin their own rise and fall, a responding beat to his rhythm.

He's right, I haven't.

I've just crossed a line I swore I never would. Problem was, I hadn't realised I was already so far over that line and living in total ignorance, pretending I wasn't quite as fucked up as I'm now positive I am.

I can't find my beast anywhere—perhaps I've scared her off? I hope she turns up later, I'm going to need her tonight.

Tilting my hips further, I show Kroe exactly what my vagina's craving, and he obliges, slipping his fingers into me in a gentle, thrusting motion that soothes my insides while softly building that surging wave of pleasure.

"You smell so sweet. I love fucking you with my fingers. Do you like this?"

A small moan escapes my lips.

He pulls his fingers out, licks them, and slips them back inside me in one smooth, subtle motion. It's almost too much for my little courtesan mind to manage.

"You taste so good. I can taste how close you are to coming for me. I want to put my tongue inside you, lick you straight from the pot ..."

Does he mean my *vagina*? Nobody's ever done that to me before...

Fucking hell.

That's exactly where I'm going—hell. Because I'm fucking enjoying this. He's never been so tender with me, *never*. I wish he'd be rough, it's easier for me to hate him when he's rough.

His fingers withdraw but then his mouth is upon me. I gasp into the sheets, clenching them in my fists while he works me over with his tongue like he knows what the fuck he's doing. I don't know what to make of it because my vagina loves it, but my heart's screaming for him to stop.

For this monster to stop doing this intimate fucking thing to me.

He thrusts his tongue inside me, lapping me up before shifting his attention to my clit, suckling it delicately, flicking it with his tongue...

I can't take this much longer. My plan was to fuck *him* into a pulp, not the other way around, while he also fucks with my head.

He needs to stop this. He fucks rough; he needs to put his penis in me and slap me back to reality before I lose both my testicles *and* my mind in one foul swoop.

"Fuck me, Kroe. Put your fucking cock inside me!" I just spoke out of turn, but he doesn't seem to care as he devours me with renewed vigour, my hips rising from the bed for him as I thrust myself into his face, because my mind may know what needs to happen here but my body's too busy enjoying herself.

The heat is building, a flame in my core spreading further with each thrust, each pump of his tongue ... until I can't hold on any longer.

I moan like the monster I am as the orgasm tears through my body, curling my toes and conscience, right before I shed a fucking tear.

Fuck this man, I fucking hate him. I do ... but he loves me in his own sick and twisted way, the only way he probably knows how to love.

He's sliding into me and I groan as my still clenching channel shifts to accommodate him. Thankfully, he starts to fuck me like he always has; hard, fast, and painfully as food and cutlery scatter across the floor. He even smacks me around a bit to remind me he's still the same old sardine eating prick.

My vagina loves it because she's a randy hoe who has a

kink for being conquered, but I fucking hate it. And that's the important thing.

But as the orgasms tear through my body, one by one ... as I put on the best fucking act of my entire life to keep him going for longer than ever, until he's so spent that he can barely form coherent speech, I start to think that it's not Kroe I actually hate ...

It's me.

Later, as Kroe snores soundly beside me, I hear the distant sound of scraping ... as though a loosened bar is being removed from a grate. I picture the girls climbing one by one through the gap—one, two, three ... on and on until I hear another sound, similar to the first but with more urgency this time, more of a thrust than a grind.

They're rushing now, with freedom but a breath away.

I lay still, my nerves thickening, rolling against my conscience as I picture what it is I'm about to do.

Shifting my hand beneath the mattress, I run my finger along the hilt of the blade.

Fuck.

Part of me had hoped it wouldn't be there—the fucked up part of me that's bound to the man lying next to me.

But no, Leila pulled through. The girls trusted her, more than they've ever trusted me.

She did this, not me. Leila ... she's a true leader.

Me ... right now? I'm a broken mess.

I need my beast, but she's abandoned me altogether.

Fuck you beast, my vagina pulled through, why can't you?

Sliding the blade from beneath the mattress, I urge it into my palm, having to move slowly, working around Kroe's hand that's clamped on my wrist. Quick movements could wake him, then I'd be dead. Instead of him.

Slow, so fucking slow ...

The blade shines in the light of the stars, glinting as I bring it down to his throat.

He looks so peaceful in his sleep ... I could almost lead myself to believe he's kind. That he cares about me in the way I always wished he had, rather than the way that came easy to him.

Do it Dell, fucking do it.

My hand's trembling. A tear paves a trail down my cheek. Moving the blade closer to his throat, I grit my teeth to prevent them from chattering, holding my breath as my entire body listens to my fucking heart, which is crying out like I'm about to murder *her*.

I close my eyes, sending more tears scattering down my cheeks.

Fuck you, heart. *Fuck you.*

Slowly, so slowly, I return the blade to its spot beneath the mattress.

A silhouette, tall, strong, familiar, stands at the open balcony doors.

Drake.

I shake my head and another tear slides down my cheek, a rush of relief enveloping me as I lower myself back to the pillow.

I've used myself time and again, my perception of myself slowly fragmenting with every conscious decision to play the fucking part.

This is where I belong.

Drake doesn't step inside the room, but he does stand there, with me, until I finally fall asleep.

CHAPTER EIGHT

The first thing I notice when Kroe drags me downstairs by my wrist, after receiving a frantic message from one of the guards that sent him flying out of bed naked, is that there aren't any girls around.

He's still pulling on his pants. Me, however, I'm butt naked. Not even my scar is hidden, though I've been forced to become a bit desensitised to that lately.

Bleary-eyed guards rush from dorm room to dorm room in search of all of Kroe's missing vaginas. Good luck, fuckers, they're long gone by now. Kroe wouldn't risk reporting it either, not after that very poignant warning to 'keep his bitches on a tighter leash' at my public whipping.

They eventually find twelve girls, perhaps ones who were too afraid to leave, or who were too far gone to survive the trip. Some of the girls might actually enjoy it here, I guess that's also a possibility—everyone has their own kinks. I just hope they weren't left behind by accident.

I'd been silently hoping to be the only one left; the Captain Vagina who goes down with the ship, or some shit.

Heroic, I know.

Kroe continues to curse the guards who look like they're still half asleep.

I'm barely hearing anything right now, barely registering time passing. I think a part of me is dying, maybe an important part.

At some point he drags me up the stairs, into his bedroom, stands me up against the wall and, without warning, backhands me across the face, the emerald ring he wears on his 'fuck you' finger slicing along my cheek.

I grab at my face, reeling from the assault.

He's panting as he lifts my chin with a harsh hand, straining my neck, forcing me to look him in the eye and huffing gross morning breath all over my face. "What do you know?"

I just want this to be over. I'm fucking done.

"They're long gone," I purr.

He lifts his hand to hit me again and at the same time a gush of blood red vomit sprays from my mouth, cascading like a waterfall to the perfectly white carpet. He kicks my legs out from under me and I fall face first into it. I feel the press of his knees on my lower back and the vicious tug of his hand in my hair, arching my neck away from the ground. Then the sharp sensation of a blade on my throat.

This is it, it's all lead to this.

There's an urgent knock on the door; loud and demanding. "Sir, members of the High Legion are here to speak with you. They found something you might find of interest."

We don't move for a second. Two. Three. Ten. Then he's pulling the knife away, getting off my back. I'm gasping for air, trying not to pass out even though right now, that would be really fucking lovely.

"I'll deal with you later." He drags me to my feet, through to the bathroom, where he wets a cloth and dabs at my face, wiping most of the blood away with a deft hand. I wish he would leave it, it's the only thing I've got covering me now, providing me with any sense of dignity.

He leads me down the stairs, towards the two waiting legionnaires with their red fucking wings puckered high, amongst a sea of men who are all fighting for the rights of the twelve vaginas left in the establishment. The girls are going to be tired by the end of the day … we all are. A small hoard of sleepy vaginas.

"Kroe, a camel has been reported roaming Hind Meadow," says the blonde one with piercing green eyes. "It was stacked high with supplies and contraband clothing. Do you have any idea about what it might've been used for?"

I'm trying to speak, because a quick death would be better than a drawn out one, and these legionaries would certainly provide that if I admit to being responsible for the loss of so many women, but I can't fucking talk! I can't even open my mouth …

I know this feeling; I've had it before. Sol's here, and he's preventing me from talking my way into an early grave.

Bastard.

"We know nothing of that, sir. Have you checked some of the smaller establishments?"

"No, we thought we'd come to you first because you usually have your finger on the pulse of this city. Where are all your girls?"

Kroe looks around casually. "We had an outbreak, so I've sent all who were showing any symptoms into quarantine, just to be safe. I hate the thought of my herd of whores spreading any diseases about."

The legionaries nod, though the one on the left—who looks more like a black-haired bulldog, has a sinister gleam in his eyes as they catch on a small, red-haired girl with a limp, pouring drinks for the men. That's when I notice Kal, drinking in the corner and looking like a fucking regular, though he's staring at me, his sapphire eyes sombre. His beer looks like it lost its head long ago.

How long has he been sitting there for, I wonder? Surely, he has better things to do, tending to his hoard of exotic females and what not; they looked like a full-time job to me. No wonder they get all hot and heady with each other, Kal's spreading his penis duties much too thinly.

"Do one of my girls take your fancy, sir?" Kroe purrs.

That got my fucking interest.

"The small red-headed one over there."

Kroe nods. "She's yours, with my compliments."

He turns his attention to me. "Make yourself useful and drag the red-headed wench out from behind the bar."

Fuck.

I take a step towards her, but Kroe grabs my fucking arm, halting me in my tracks. "Answer me!"

Someone's in a mood this morning. I guess he's a bit sad he lost most of his pet vaginas. I swivel to face him, try to speak but ... my mouth's glued fucking *shut*.

Oh ... shit.

I make some weird muffled sound that has Kroe practically searing, hand tightening around my bicep. My eyes dart about nervously, I shuffle, pretend to scratch and then finally, my lips part dramatically and I can fucking speak again. "Yes, sir," I croak.

Kroe's fist clenches at his side and he jerks his chin in the direction of the girl. "Go. Get the man his whore." He drops his hand, leaving a bright red stain on my skin. I turn my attention back towards that mop of fiery hair.

She's small ... fragile. Her eyes are red rimmed, deep smudges beneath them that she's tried to conceal with too much powder. She has the look of someone who's lost the will to fight.

Goddammit.

I don't have the energy for another moral dilemma right now—I honestly think another one would destroy me. I've been with one of the red-winged bastards, and I can't let *her* go through that … because it would kill her in ways it possibly wouldn't kill me. Though my mind's on death's door, my body seems to cope with physical abuse better than most.

I walk to the bar, towards the young girl.

Towards Kal.

He watches me draw near, gaze not once roaming my naked body. It's admirable, it really is. Even though he looks like any regular fucker in this establishment, even though he's dressed like one … he isn't one.

He's my God of the fucking Night.

And I have one wish left.

One.

"I wish for you to fuck the red-haired girl whose standing behind the bar, now, as yourself, the God of Night," I mumble, not loud enough for anyone around me to hear, but loud enough for the fucking god right there to hear with his divine hearing abilities.

His olive skin turns a sickly shade of grey, eyes widening, studying me while I continue to stride naked towards the bar, towards the girl I just wished for him to bang.

I'm the best fucking wing-woman ever, these guys really should appreciate me for that. I've gotten at least two of them laid in the past twelve hours, and that's pretty fucking impressive considering my current circumstances. They should call me Cupid and give me a sexy little slingshot for me to shoot my whore bolts about.

I swear I look positively savage right now—perfect because if I'm walking to my death, I want to look badass doing it. My scar is on show for all to see, the one from the culling of my uterus, and I'm fucking owning it. I'm a survivor, not a victim. I made it this far and managed to save some lives along the way. Even so, I wish I had some of Kal's shit kicking boots on. They'd really give me the ultimate badass hip swing to finish off the look.

A warm wash floods over me and I feel the proverbial weight lift from my shoulders, because I've done my part. I've used all my wishes and I'm no longer dragging the wish chain. It's up to the men now.

There's a flash of light just before I reach the bar. Kal disappears, reappearing next to Kroe, wearing his sexy fucking god gear that's all black and shiny. The entire room gasps then instantly bows, including me this time. It's nice not to be tied between two giant erect cocks for a change.

Kal signals for everyone to rise as Kal and Kroe exchange words I can't hear, but all I'm really watching is the legionnaire's bulldog face as he scans the crowd, no doubt searching for another vagina who might tickle his pickle. He looks a little fucked off, though he's hiding it well. But I know men. I know their tells…

He likes small feeble women, like the scared little red-haired over there, the one Kal's now leading up the staircase, into his own private room.

Don't vomit. Don't vomit. Don't vomit.

Suddenly there's a man standing before me, a swath of white hair… a pair of pale blue eyes I know.

Sol—he's well disguised, tight jawed, fists clenched and shaking. His canines are extending longer than usual, coming down just shy of the bottom of his lower lip.

It's the first time I've looked in his eyes since the whipping, since I wished for him to bring me back to this shit hole in the first place.

My heart almost pounces out of my chest.

Fuck.

'I'm sorry,' I mouth, ignoring the way his eyes widen as he

lurches forward to grab me, before I take off through the crowd, because if that legionnaire notices another vagina before he notices *me,* then I'm all out of fucking luck. She'd probably die, because they're brutal as shit and the only vaginas left here are ones who wouldn't be able to stand the abuse, let alone survive it.

Working my way around the back of the crowd, I somehow avoid receiving an unsanctioned penis in my naked vulva, before I pop out behind the legionnaire and 'tumble' into his back like a fucking pansy, sending his wings fluttering outwards as he stumbles towards Kroe.

I peer up at him with frightened eyes, feebly pawing the air as I try to stand upright.

Kroe smooths his suit pants, skims a hand through his hair, watching me with a suspicious, narrowed gaze. But my job is done.

"I'll take this one instead," the High Fae states, with a nasty fucking quirk to his lips.

He missed me before—he hasn't now.

"That one has a prior engagement, sir," Kroe says, lifting his chin. "I'm sorry … can I interest you in—"

"No, you cannot." The legionnaire flicks Kroe a gold drab. "I won't be long." He whips his hand around my arm, half dragging me up the stairs, Kroe following closely at our heels, obviously not wanting to lose tabs on his little cupcake vagina.

This was a real great idea. I'm full of them lately.

I think I'm imagining things when I spot a swathe of gold, curly hair in the crowd below, before we reach the second floor and I'm pulled into an empty suite. The door is slammed in Kroe's face.

I guess he wants to make sure I don't crawl out the window after I've been fucked seven ways sideways, but I doubt I'll have the ability to even move once we're done, if my instincts prove correct.

The legionnaire tosses me onto the ground and I slam against the dresser next to the bed, feeling a sharp pain as something cracks in my abdomen.

"How does a would-be breeder end up as a whore, that's what I want to know," he spits, leaning over me.

I try to answer but the only sound that comes out is a groan. I'm pretty sure he just snapped something important.

"Answer me, whore!"

"I don't know ..."

He spits at me, a thick wad that lands on my cheek. "You probably fucking asked for it. You like cock so much you couldn't bear the thought of having only one every twelve months or so, eh? You're all the fucking same, gagging for dick like the filth you are."

He picks me up by my neck and I'm hanging like a rag doll before him. "Tell me, slut, how many cocks have you had in your life?"

I claw at my neck, unable to breath, let alone answer his ridiculous question.

Hissing, he heaves me against the stone wall. The impact rips the air from my lungs and I crumble in a heap at its base, managing to drag in a single, shuddering breath before he hauls me out by my feet, flips me over, pushes my legs apart and unbuttons his trousers. He spits on his hand before lathering himself up with his own saliva, and sheaths himself in me.

My body grinds backwards and forwards along the unforgiving floor, peeling skin off my limbs, painting the floor with my blood. His hand comes up to my head, forcing my face into the stone and having the same effect on the sharp of my right cheekbone.

I don't know if I can come back from this.

I don't know if I *want* to come back from this.

I blank in and out of consciousness as he hammers into me, over and over.

Finally, when there is nothing else, all I see are feathers.

Fucking feathers, I fucking hate them. I never want to see another feather again.

He empties himself inside me, hands around my neck, squeezing, squeezing until he's spent. Then he leaves, walking out the door and slamming it shut behind him.

I can't move, can barely breathe.

I'm so fucking alone.

I don't want to die alone.

Shouldn't Kroe be sauntering in right now to whack himself off over the sight of my blood?

I'm barely aware of a flash of white light blanketing the room, then I'm being peeled off the ground by gentle hands. "I've got you, baby. I'm not letting go."

Aero.

He tugs me close and I let out a groan as all the emotions flood to the surface in a singular, heart-wrenching wave.

Another flash of white has me passing out entirely.

CHAPTER NINE

*H*e told me he wouldn't let me go, and by the looks of things, he hasn't. It's my first thought when I wake, submerged in the covers of the rose rock bed at my tower in the Dawn Kingdom, Aero sleeping next to me on my left side, one arm cocooning my head, the other wrapped around my left arm, fingers splayed against my cheek.

Kal, also sleeping, is horizontal to me, my legs across his lap, his head bent to rest against one foot which he's holding in his cupped hands. Drake's on my right side, holding my hand, his head nestled against my shoulder.

My heart starts to race … pounding so hard I'm sure the fucker's going to explode. As nice and as cosy as this is, I'm panicking.

Get yourself under control, Dell.

My breathing thickens and I'm gasping, eyes darting everywhere, over the bandages covering my body, around the room, clawing at the dark world beyond the windows … coming to rest on the God of Day sitting on a seat before the fire hearth, watching me.

He looks like he's barely breathing, his face unreadable,

but his hands are wrapped tightly around the arms of the chair as the firelight licks at his perfect, godly features.

Moments pass, the only sound that of my fragile, beating heart ... as we absorb each other, silently, our unsaid words driving a distance between us that I can't face right now. I can't face *him*.

I try to move, crying out as a shaft of pain slices through my abdomen. Sol grips the chair so hard it actually fucking groans. Aero pulls me tighter towards him, eliciting another strangled sound from my throat. Someone needs to peel the dawn vice off my broken bits.

Aero loosens his hold and sits up. The other two rouse instantly, worried expressions clinging to my every inch.

"I need ... I need space ..." I gasp, amidst laboured breaths.

My limbs are freed, my Gods jumping back off the bed. I bring my hands to my face, rubbing my palms over it and wincing at the still-raw wounds on my cheeks. "How many?"

"How many what?"

"The girls! *How many?*" I can't get enough breath, I can't look at them, I can't fucking *think straight*.

It's Sol who answers, from where he's now standing, near the hearth. "Fifty-seven. You saved fifty-seven females."

The lump that forms in my throat threatens to choke me. Fifty-seven, but twelve are left behind.

I left *twelve* behind.

Aero shifts in closer, perching himself on the edge of the bed. "Don't fucking think like that. You *saved* those girls, Dell. The ones left behind either knew they were dying or that their bodies would never make the trip. The rest had lost the will to live."

Daring to look him in the eye, I catch a glimpse of the depth of his emotion, which I choose to ignore. I can't deal with that right now.

"I had lost the will to live. Why the fuck do I deserve to be here when they're still stuck in that hell hole being treated like than fucking dirt?"

I need to get them out.

I start inching my way out of bed, my arm plastered over my midsection. It'll take me years at this rate, but by the time I get there I'll probably be well enough to help.

Kal clears his throat. "Day?"

And now I can't move at all, my body laying back down without my permission to fucking do so.

Fuck you, Sol.

I lay there, unmoving, as the bottled-up emotion finally surges out of me in great, heaving sobs, tears which I can't seem to stop once they start. They're certainly not regular tears; the ones you can't hear but you can see … no, these are tears that rip your soul open and bear it to the world. The ones that make you feel like you're not in control of your life, or make you realise that you never were in the first place. That much is true for me, anyway, because I can't let go of the past. It just keeps coming back to haunt me, and I'm so fucking inadequate that I could only get fifty-seven girls free, when an entire *world* of them are suffering.

Warm hands caress my face, and I don't mind. I've just realised I'm too far gone for it to really matter anymore.

"Shhh. It's okay." Kal smooths the hair from my face. "It's okay."

It's not though, it's not okay at all.

At some point Gail comes in and sets some food on a table. My Gods insist I eat something, which leads to Kal hand feeding me little hard-boiled eggs.

Gail looks less than impressed when she returns an hour later and realises the platters have barely been touched, but my mind's not on food right now—it's on the thick wad of fuckery I just swam through naked.

I'm angry. Disappointed. Because even though I saved a small hoard of women, I didn't exactly achieve it in admirable style.

"I used myself." I'm looking straight out the window, into the shadows I belong in. It makes sense ... to be raised in the darkness, what else should I expect than to become the darkness myself?

"You did what you had to do." Kal says it as if he's putting a full stop on the conversation, but I'm not even close to done.

The others are murmuring between themselves, having their own private conversation I'm apparently not privy to.

"I enjoyed some of it, Kal." Yeah, now the room is really fucking quiet. "Maybe I'm just as bad as them."

"You're a survivor. Your body did what it had to do, to survive."

"Because I can't control the bitch."

"You underestimate yourself, Dell ..."

I don't. I know my body, know its strengths and weaknesses. They won't always see me as a survivor—a little mortal body can only hold its own through the shit I've been through for so fucking long. But I don't tell him that, choosing instead to marinate in my dark world where I'm just as bad as the fuckers who screw me daily. My mind was rotten well before the Sun Gods met me.

Time drips by in glorious mind-fucking silence. Kal slowly shuffles himself further onto the bed; inch by inch, until only a hair's breadth separates us. I realise how exhausted I am, how little fight I have left in me. Even if I *could* move my traitorous body right now, I wouldn't have the energy to run.

Not that I'd make it far without wings. I'd have to rely on my Kingdom of penis serpents to taxi me back to the mainland. Not that I can speak penis serpent. That would've been an interesting excursion with very little traction.

The three others are coagulated by the hearth, still speaking in hushed tones too quiet for my fantastic hearing to make out. Having a good old Sun God pow wow, it seems.

Conversation apparently over, Sol strides to the balcony door without looking back, and throws himself off the side of the building, into the night beyond.

I let out a shuddering sigh. There's so much unsaid between us, and now he's gone.

At least I can move now that he's not here. I rub at my chest to try and ease the pain in my heart.

"You should sleep, Dell," says Kal. "Your emotions are up and down ... even I can't keep up."

I look up at the rose rock roof, and only now see the giant fucking hole in it.

Wow.

Aero gave my tower its own fucking skylight? It's half the size of the roof!

I wonder what happens when it rains? Actually, no, I don't care. I'm *beyond* impressed. I'll dance naked in that rain.

I draw a deep breath, then slowly push it out. "I'm worried that if I go to sleep, I'll wake back there again." I stare at the stars, swallow back the tears threatening to spill again. "I thought I'd die there."

"You're here, you're safe. We're not going to let anything like that happen to you again."

Shaking my head, I trail the brightness of the stars, studying the darkness that threatens to absorb them. "I'm realising more and more that fate works in really fucked up ways. I'm not immortal, Kal. I'm going to die. I've had a long time to get used to the fact." I turn my face to the side and look him in the eye. "You can't protect me from all the monsters. You can't protect me from myself."

His brow crinkles and he plucks a curl from my bandaged cheek. "You're not a monster, you've just been exposed to a world of men who can't control their own."

I shake my head. "The things I did in there ..."

"You saved the lives of fifty-seven girls. You got out *alive*."

I study his face, the high arc of his cheekbones, long dark lashes framing his eyes and the way his well-defined cupid's bow flows perfectly into full lips. He's one sexy man god, I'll hand him that.

"I'm not entirely convinced I *am* alive. Not properly."

I turn my attention back to the sky, the stars, the nothingness overhead.

I mean what I said, even my vagina's fucked off entirely. I tried to picture Kal's lips becoming acquainted with my labia and she didn't even blink a vulva.

My beast is nowhere to be seen ... probably because I'm frightened of her and she knows it. Probably because her presence reminds me of all the horrible things I've done over the past two weeks, chewing penises off and what not.

Perhaps she's ashamed.

A mental picture of the severed cock flashes through my mind, and I can't sit up quick enough, groaning because my body's complaining like the weak bitch it is.

"What is it?"

"What's wrong?"

"I'm going to be sick," I manage to grind out, and Drake grabs my wrist, flashing me straight to the bathroom and directly in front of the toilet bowl.

He's standing over me, pulling my fucking hair back. The gesture's so sweet it makes my stomach churn even harder. I can't deal with sweet right now.

I signal for him to *get the fuck out*, but he hesitates, finally conceding when I throw a toilet brush at him. I reach my leg out and push the door shut with a loud slam before hurling my guts into the toilet bowl, splattering the sides and filling the bowl with blood.

A lot of it.

"Shit …" that's a lot of red.

"*Dell*? I'm coming in."

"Double shit." I flush the evidence away before Aero can catch a glimpse of it himself, slapping the lid down right before he storms the fucking door. I stare the ruthless bastard down from my spot in front of the toilet. "Don't you know *anything* about personal boundaries?"

He paces straight to the toilet, opening the lid and taking a peek inside the bowl. "I do, I just don't give a fuck about them right now. What was that about blood?"

"My gums are bleeding. I haven't brushed in days."

He's looking at me, looking at me still, yup … still looking at me. Wish he'd just point me in the direction of the toothbrushes and give me some personal space before I have a mental fucking breakdown.

His expression softens and he drags a stool over to the vanity then helps me stand, supporting me while I shuffle towards it. He prepares a toothbrush with some white tooth jizz then turns to leave the room. "Call when you're done. Don't try and come back out here by yourself, I don't want you falling over and breaking something."

Aye aye, Captain Big Cock. I'm not sure why he's so worried about me breaking his house, it's made of fucking rose rock.

"I mean your bones, Dell, for fuck's sake … you can crumble this place to the ground for all I care!" he bellows from behind the closed door.

"Oh …" Oops.

I brush the blood from my teeth and mouth, ignoring the mirror the whole time. I'm not entirely sure who it is I'll see looking back at me right now.

Using the lavatory proves to be painful, but I'm thankful for that. All my other wounds are numbed; I'm glad they didn't bother to numb my arsehole and vagina because I would've been really pissed if they had. My late vagina may have been fanging for these men, but even *she* would've been pissed off if they got a tickle in while she was passed the fuck out.

When I finally call for them, it's Drake who returns for me.

"Hi…" I say from the safety of my stool.

"Hi … sorry, fuck. I'm not very good at keeping my distance right now."

"It's fine." I wave my hand at him, ushering him closer. "I just needed some space. Sorry about the shit brush."

He kneels in front of me and I can see by the look in his eyes that he wants to say something. He's probably trying to find the right words to broach said subject with a tortured whore who bit a guy's penis off. Problem is, I'm completely against being led in conversation right now.

"How did you get me out?" I ask, just as he opens his mouth to speak.

He swallows his words. "Ah … fuck, it wasn't easy with so many wards to work around, plus we're weak as shit at the moment."

"That's what I mean, how did you get me alone? Kroe was waiting outside the door for us to finish, he wasn't willing to let me out of his sight after I disappeared for so long…"

Drake nods. "I know, that was the problem. We had to find a way to both subtly *and* strategically distract him from coming into the room straight after the red-winged fucker left, so it couldn't be pinpointed to us, set off the wards and fucking kill us."

Obviously. Am I imagining things or is the bastard jumping around the point?

"So … how'd you do it, Drake?"

He looks positively guilty—avoiding my eye contact as he draws a deep breath, lets it out and shrugs. "Started a fire."

"You … you *what*? Are you fucking *insane*?"

I'm now picturing the entire place in ruins, charred bodies left right and centre. Those poor women, the ones who couldn't make the trip because they were too injured or broken to leave. And their payment? Getting roasted alive by my fucking Sun Gods!

"Babe, calm down … I know it's been your home, but it's just a fucking brothel!"

"Don't fucking tell me to be calm!" I'm ready to shed some fucking Dusk blood. I wonder if it runs gold?

"Is everyone okay in there?" Aero hollers from the door, making me hiss like a savage.

Drake looks nervous, like he actually wants to open that door and request backup. I level him with a death stare and watch the bastard gulp.

"Unless you want your balls roasted too, Aero, I suggest you leave that fucking door closed!"

I hear nothing more from my Dawn God. Clever man.

Drake sighs. "It wasn't his idea, Dell …"

I get that he's trying to own his shit, and that's admirable, but I'm still fucked off.

"So, it was yours?"

He nods.

"Lovely. Just fucking lovely. How could you do that?" I plead scream because I can't make up my mind if I'm pleading or screaming. And the fucker has the gall to roll his fucking eyes at me!

I thought more of this man. I really did. I'm so disappointed in myself right now. I'm so disappointed in *him*.

"I'll say it again, it's just a fucking brothel. It was only a small fire, fucking hell. It was the only shot we had, we were running out of options, Dell! You were fucking dying!"

I'm still dying, I'm a fucking mortal, but I don't think now's the right time to bring that up. I draw a couple of deep, uneven breaths, filling my lungs as I prepare myself to ask the question I'm dreading the answer to. "How many people died in the blaze? How many of my girls?"

"*Died?*"

"Yes! How fucking many?"

"None! Kroe had it smothered within about three minutes."

Ahh.

Right.

Well then ... I mull over that for a second, replaying the conversation in my head and concluding that I acted like a total fucking crazy bitch. Awkward.

"So, in other words, I ..."

"Overreacted? I think that's the word you're looking for." He throws me a half smile that my vagina would've gobbled right up, had she been present and accounted for. Bastard shouldn't have acted so fucking guilty at the start.

"Sorry. I thought you fried my friends."

"And why the fuck would we do that? We needed to get you out, yes, but we would never let anyone underserving die in the fucking process." He frowns, studying me far too intently at such a close proximity. "Is that what you really think of me?"

Oh dear, communication is hard work. Maybe I was better off without permission to speak? In my defence, I haven't had a great deal of practise at this shit.

I sigh. "No Drake, it's not ... granted I *used* to think that of you *all*, but my opinions have changed significantly since then."

"Good. Fucking hell."

I rub my face with the palm of my hand. "Relationships are hard work."

He cocks a brow at me. "I couldn't agree more."

I ignore that rude little comment and clear my throat. "How much ... how much did you guys *see* in there?"

Drake shuffles uncomfortably, rubbing at his face, calluses scratching against golden stubble. "Ahh ... you're probably not going to like this, but we always had someone watching you, looking for an opportunity to get you on your own."

Fuck.

"*Always?*" I choke on the word.

"Yeah ..."

Good god. So they definitely saw me chew that guys penis off. I'm surprised Aero was able to get an erection around me. Not to mention all the fuckery they saw ...

"Aero relayed the parts of your plan he knew, which fucked me right off. Well, all of us. I'm not sure what you thought you had to fucking *prove* to them. We kept looking for opportunities to get you out."

"It wasn't about '*proving*' anything, Drake. It was more than that."

He shakes his head. "I don't want to hear it, and I don't want to talk about that right now. It'll just make me break something and I'm not in the fucking mood. And you're not in the right condition for me to lay into you about the importance of self-preservation." He pins me with a glare. "Even though I'd fucking *love* to lay into you right now."

I feel like there's a greater meaning to that comment that my vagina would've fucking bathed in.

He breaks our eye contact and shakes his head. "We considered paying Kroe for a private show just to get you out of there, even though you would've grumbled loud enough to make a fucking scene."

"I definitely would've."

He growls under his breath and mumbles something that sounds suspiciously like 'I need to fuck some sense into you,' though I can't be certain …

"Kroe would've realised it was us who took you anyway, and the wards would've kicked in." He swipes a droplet of blood from my arm, frowning at it, then wipes it on a towel.

Should've checked myself over for backlash, whoops.

"And then he chained you to that girl, making it even more difficult because we can't touch iron; and it meant you were never alone, not even on the fucking pisser."

"Leila."

Drawing in a deep breath, I think about the girl who helped me in more ways than she will ever know. If I ever see her again, I swear I'm going to praise her on how ruthlessly she plunged that guys arsehole with her arm. Fucking brilliant. I'll take that vision to my grave, treasuring it fondly.

Perhaps not so much the vision of Aero's penis plunging deep inside her vagina, though it was a turn on at the time. It probably would've been sexier if I wasn't getting banged to a pulp by a crazy fucker who bit me.

Aero growls from the next room.

'Calm your sausage!'

Clearing my throat, I say out loud, "Aero fucked her."

That growl turns into a choking sound.

Drake's brow crinkles. "He did … but he should've sent me to do that. I have more control than he does."

Meaning he wanted to fuck Leila. Just lovely. Not going to lie though, if I batted for the other team, I'd totally be all up in that twat myself. I huff out a humourless laugh. "Seemed like he did just fine to me."

Drake shakes his head. "No, Dell. He should have taken her to another room. You didn't need to see that."

At the time, I kind of did. It was like a dab of Sun God porn, but I don't think I should say that.

"So, you would've what ... taken her to another room and fucked her there instead?"

Drake smiles, though it doesn't reach his eyes. "I wouldn't have fucked her at all babe, not with my cock. I would've taken her to a room, plastered her face first over the side of one of those sex couches, hoisted her arse in the air and I would've gone to town on her clit. Perhaps even fucked her with my tongue a bit while I slipped a finger in her arse and given her the best orgasm of her entire shitty existence."

Holy Dusk babies.

I just need a moment.

His attention dips to the bandage on my neck. "Fucking wanker, that guy needs to be castrated. Aero almost tore his throat out, but Sol compelled him to stand the fuck still."

Ahh...

"What?"

Drake shrugs. "Told you it should've been me. Big dose of wasted energy right there."

Fucking hell. These Sun Gods, they're a full-time gig. Not to mention I seem to be costing them significantly ... at this rate, they'll be lucky to break even once they finally use their fucking wishes on me.

I give the wound a little prod and wince at the resonating pain. "It should've healed by now."

"It won't for a while. It's a mating bite."

"A ... *what?*" My body goes limp and I feel myself drifting to the side ... Drake grasps my shoulders, stopping me from falling head the fuck first onto the pretty rose rock ground that probably gives harder than it takes.

"You okay?"

No, I'm not fucking okay. "Explain!"

"Ahh ... the practice has begun to fade out over the years,

particularly for Lesser Fae. Subsequently, the venom is gradually weakening in your new generations, though the biology's still the same. If you had bitten the fucker back while his venom was still in your system, you would've been mated for life to that toad."

No.

Fucking.

Way.

"Holy shit balls."

Drake nods. "Yeah ..."

Thank fuck I didn't retaliate. I probably would've bitten his cock had he put it in my mouth after the way he treated me, and then I would've been mated to his rank fucking penis for the rest of my goddamn life. Dodged a self-induced lobotomy, there!

Come to think of it, I'll never bite someone's penis again. If Ballsack Two had survived somehow with his half penis, and bitten me back, I could've been mated to that fucker too. Wow, what a shitty existence that would've been. No g-spot orgasms for me!

"Ok, enough bathroom talk. This shit's heavy." He helps me stand, then I give him a little nudge to tell my overbearing Dusk God I need to do this on my own, wincing as I shuffle forward a few steps before stubbing my toe on the corner of the ornate fucking vanity. Bastard, I swear it moved mid-step.

I swallow my pride and stop trying to walk, mainly because I'm doing a shit job of it anyway. "Can you carry me?"

Drake eyes my outstretched arms, probably waiting for me to change my mind, complicated bitch that I am, before he lifts me into his arms. I breathe in his smell, warm and dusky at once, like a rainbow at golden hour. I take another whiff and he laughs as we cross the room back to the bed. I notice Kal and Aero still chatting quietly by the fire, but still no sign of my Day God.

"Where's Sol gone?"

"Fucked off."

I roll my eyes. "Yeah, no shit. Where too?"

Drake shrugs. "He's got business to attend, fields to plough, that sort of thing."

Fucking hell, Drake's let his inner teenager come out to play again. My vagina would've had a field day with that if she were still with us. Rest in peace.

"*Aero*! Where's Sol gone?"

"You don't have to yell at me, Dell. I have direct access to your thoughts." He saunters towards the bed, leaving Kal mulling over the flames like he's got the world on his shoulders.

"I know, but I haven't had many chances to talk over the past week and I missed the sound of my voice."

"Ploughing fields, little mortal. He's got business to attend."

"Exactly what I fucking said!" Drake's looking at me like he's offended I didn't trust him in the first place.

Great. Lovely. Sol and I have unspoken ground to cover and he's off relieving his blue balls.

Fucking swell.

Good thing I'm patient ... most of the time. I have a God to apologise to.

CHAPTER TEN

Red feathers. So many red fucking feathers.
I try to move, to get away, but I'm pinned to the spot. I scream but it comes out a strangled gurgle. There's a hand around my throat, squeezing, squeezing … I can't breathe.

I claw at him, battling for release, but he's thrusting into me at the same time, every impalement crushing my windpipe, bringing me closer to death's fucking doorway.

I'm useless.

Powerless …

Bile stains my throat and that sadistic gleam only engorges my fear. "What's in your box, little mortal?"

Panic. Pure undiluted panic. I can't breathe, *can't breathe*!

"Dell!"

Aero's voice drags me back to the now, to my bed which is soaked through with sweat, tears, and blood.

I'm panting, hot, too fucking hot.

Aero's pulling me into a seating position, but I can't get enough air.

We flash into the Bright then out again, and suddenly

we're waist deep in an indoor pool. Aero has no shirt on, not bloody helping me cool down.

Needing the weightlessness of the water and not the close confines of all this man meat, I push away from him.

"Are you okay?"

I shake my head and wade in a wide circle, trying to focus on the feel of the water against my skin. "Bad dream. Is my box safe?" My other box, not the one I'm in the process of building a pyre for.

"Yes. I hid it well."

"You didn't look in it?" I ask, narrowing my eyes at him.

He looks offended, but I need to know.

"A wish is a wish."

"Good."

He starts to speak, but I dunk beneath the surface, scrubbing at my face with the palms of my hands before surfacing to find Aero standing in front of me, his eyes shadowed, the air thickening with tension.

"I'm sorry ..."

"For what?"

He straightens his shoulders. "I should have taken Leila into a different room."

Fucking hell. I'm not sure I want to go there. "Can we just ... not do this right now?"

He shakes his head. "No. We're doing it."

"Why?"

"Because I know you fucking care."

I take a step back, then another. He follows, reaching forward and fisting my shift, halting me in place.

"Stop running."

I frown, meeting the determination in his gaze. "Fine, fuck. If you want to go there, then we'll go there. Why did you do it, Aero? There were plenty of private rooms you could have used."

Features softening, he releases a deep breath that almost looks like ... relief?

Why the fuck is he relieved?

A deep rumble emanates from his chest. "I couldn't leave you. Not with that man fantasising about sinking his fucking teeth into your neck."

"You knew he wanted to do that?"

"I could hear him thinking about it, yes."

"Were you worried I'd bite him back and mate with the bastard?"

Aero reels me in further, coaxing me with the hand still clutched to my shift. I try to ignore the fact that he smells so fucking good.

"It was more than that. I can't lie though, that was certainly part of it."

I growl at him—It isn't pretty. "I would *never* have bitten that fucker ... like that."

Aero shrugs, looking entirely unperturbed by my little show of aggression. "Even Lesser venom can be compelling. It gets into your system and floods you with a haze of lust. Besides, those teeth of yours seem to have a mind of their own ..."

Fucking hell. Is he talking about my penis biting experience?

I pull away, but he tugs me closer, until we're chest to fucking chest and I'm heaving angry air all over his glistening, honey skin.

"Stop trying to fucking run from me. I told you, I'm not letting you go." He lifts his free hand, running wet knuckles along the base of my jaw. "My point is, I lost control. You didn't need to see that."

Studying the beads of water littering his chest, I almost smile. "At the time, I kind of did." I lift my gaze to his, recognising the heat in his eyes as that smile finally tugs at the corner of my mouth. "But you knew that already."

He blinks, and that heat is gone—replaced with a steel resolve that dissolves my smile instantly. "Still—I'm sorry, Adeline."

I take a step back, my features melting at the sound of my full name coming from his lips. "You know it?"

"I heard it. I like it…"

"I don't." It's a lie. I do, it just hurts to hear it.

"I won't use it then."

Turning away, I almost start to cry, fuck it. I distract myself from my errant emotions by looking around the place.

This tower is hewn from red-stone, most of the wall space made up of wide opened windows.

"Your tower?" I look over my shoulder at Aero, who's eyeing me like I'm some feeble animal that might try to flap off with half a wing and a broken spine. Do I really look that pathetic?

"It is and no, you don't." He wades closer. "I'm just … I'm feeling things I've never felt before."

I submerge fully, because I'm not sure how to respond to that, but I obviously take too long to come back up because he's suddenly right next to me, easing me back to the surface by my underarms, wiping my face with smooth, gentle strokes of his hands. He dips his head to meet my gaze, his hair flopping forward and casting a shadow over his eyes. "This is my personal tower. I've never brought anyone here before…"

I try to dunk again but he's holding me up, looking at me … into me.

Shit.

"These conversations are making me uncomfortable."

"I can tell."

"Where are the others?" I ask, subtly changing the subject. I'm sure it came off that way, too.

"Ploughing fields with Sol."

Fucking hell. Kinky fucking Sun Gods. I don't know who the women are, but I'll cut the bitches.

Yikes. Calm down, crazy cucumber. You're a Lesser Fae whore with a dead vagina. They're Sun Gods, with … needs. I try to swallow the tang of … jealousy? Good god, what's happening to me?

Pushing myself away, I make for the deeper part of the pool that should hopefully go over my head.

"Dell …"

"Calm down, I'm not going to drown myself."

But he follows me, diving beneath the water and coming up in front of me, glistening and disgustingly perfect.

He lets out the breath he was holding and wipes the excess water from his face. "You're not strong enough yet, you need to take it slowly."

I roll my eyes, try to move past him, but he catches me in his arms, pulling me close again, mixing breath, branding me with his gaze.

"You don't have to do that with me."

"Do what?" I try to push away, he only holds me tighter.

"Pretend like you don't give a fuck."

"I'm *programmed* not to give a fuck."

He shakes his head and his hand grasps my shift, keeping me at bay like the rogue bitch I am. My vagina would've loved this. Though he's frowning at me now … rumbling a little.

"No, you're not. You're programmed to repress your baser urges because you think they make you a monster; someone just as bad as the men who've fucked you, the *man* who fucked you daily since you were far too young to understand what the *fuck* was going on."

Fucking hell.

I push at his chest, trying to get away, but he won't let me go. "You've been listening this whole time ..."

"I miss nothing." He pushes the words through his teeth and his face inches closer. "*Nothing*"

"You've got something on your mind, spit it out, Aero! You think you know me so well then surely you know I hate it when people pussyfoot around shit."

He shakes his head and I can feel his muscles bunching beneath his skin, can see his pupils expanding, suffocating the molten amber. "No, you hate it when people show they care because in your mind, Dell, if someone cares they're going to hurt you. So you isolate yourself; thinking you can take on your demons by yourself, but below the surface we're all the same, craving a familiar touch that gives us validation. You're right where he wants you. That man has had you on a string this entire ... fucking ... time."

Wow. Just ... wow.

"That's rich coming from a fucking sadist. *Let me go*," I hiss, and he does, my shift unfurling from his grasp.

I push towards the edge of the pool that doubles as an infinity window. By the time I reach the orgasmic view across the cityscape—cylindrical spires crowding the horizon and bathed in sunlight—I'm gasping for breath, and not in the good way. I can feel him behind me, though he's as silent as an unexpected erection popping up to say hello.

"So, you've realised how fucked up I am, good for you."

The water shifts about me as he wades closer. "You're not the first person to fall in love with their captor."

I turn and he's right there, so close I can't see past him. I would have to arch my neck to catch his eye contact, so instead I stare at his conveniently placed pectoral muscles. "I'm not in love with him, I just can't seem to kill the fucker."

He places one hand on the side of the pool, boxing me in

to the right but leaving the left as an escape route. I see his intention; I can get away if I want to, I'm not his prisoner.

His free hand comes up to my chin, tilting my head, though I do everything in my power to avoid looking the sexy bastard in the eye.

"Look at me, Dell."

I try, I really do. I keep dragging my eyes closer to his face, then darting them away again because I can't handle ...

"Dell, please." He's pinching my chin between his thumb and forefinger. It starts to hurt. Gritting my teeth, I finally look the fucker in the eye.

"There you are ..."

I swallow, pressing myself further against the smooth stone behind me, doing my best to create a semblance of space between us. "What do you see?"

He reaches up, tucking a sodden, wayward curl behind my ear. "I see ..." He shakes his head, drawing a deep breath then settling himself closer to me, before letting it out—a warm brush against my face. "I see a woman bound, but one who is *boundless*. I see the beast inside you Dell, and I fucking *love* her."

I feel the blood drain from my face and my body goes limp, right before his lips crush into mine.

I stumble from the hit I wasn't expecting, but my shock is overwhelmed because his lips are warm, soft and sensual as they work over my inexperienced ones—not hard and rough like I expected them to be.

I don't know what to fucking do, I've never done this before. This is new territory for me ...

Instinct takes hold and I open my mouth to him, allowing his tongue to slip between my teeth and gently caress my own. It's tentative at first, like he's tasting me, testing my limitations.

The hand that was holding my chin shifts around the

back of my head, pressing me further into him as he delves deeper into my mouth. I let out a moan because it feels so fucking good. He tastes like dawn personified; sweet, bright and *alive*.

He brings his other hand around and threads it across my back, pressing my body closer to his and exposing me to every muscle and rivet, and they are ample.

Sweet baby Dawnies. My vagina rises from the grave like a fucking phoenix reborn.

I thread my hands through his hair, devouring him as he groans into my mouth.

I've never heard a man make sounds quite like that, like he's actually enjoying *me*, and not just the *idea* of me, a little 'sex slave'.

Feeling brave, I slide my tongue into his mouth, exploring the territory there, including those spectacular canines that seem to have lengthened, joining the other part of him that I can also feel has become significantly longer.

I run my tongue along the tip of it; the canine I mean, not his penis—pricking myself in the process and revelling in the small sting of pain.

He retreats swifter than a man repressing his desire to have his butt fingered, leaving me gasping for more of that Aero tongue candy.

"Fuck! Show me your tongue Dell, how big is the cut?"

Huh?

I'm still panting for purchase from whatever the fuck we just did, my vagina's weeping a little happy cry that she's alive again, and he wants to inspect my fucking *tongue*?

"Yes, Dell. My venom's more potent than a Lesser, it acts a bit differently." He's forcing my mouth open with his fucking fingers as he dips and squints to inspect my mouth. Buzz kill.

"Is this really necessary?" I say around his fingers, but

then I start to sway a little ... am I about to go all limp dick on him? What an anticlimax.

He pulls his fingers from my mouth, inspecting my eyes and brushing his hand over my brow. "Shit. I'm taking you back to the room, then I'll find one of the others to take care of you for a while."

"What? Why?" I shuffle along the wall, out of his reach, gaining some sense of my balance back, though I now feel very territorial about staying *right the fuck here*. "I don't want to go *anywhere*. I'm fine where I am, thank you!"

"Baby c'mon, it's just until the venom wears off." He's edging towards me like I'm some skittish animal.

"Why? So we don't form a mating bond?" I arch a brow at him as he takes another step forward, and I take another step back.

He puts his hands up in submission. "I don't want you biting me under the influence of my venom, that's why. If you bite me, I want it to be because you *want* to fucking bite me, not because I compelled you to with my God juice."

God juice? That sounds fun.

That's when I realise I've stopped stepping back, and I'm now leaning *forward*, salivating over the sight of his neck. What the actual fuck?

"So ... you don't want me to bite you?"

"No ... I mean yes ... but no!"

"Because I want to bite you ... I want to bite you fucking everywhere. Not your cock though, just so we're clear. My career in chewing penis's off is well and truly over. Bring me your bicep, I want to bite your bicep."

"Dell, no ..."

I'm lunging for him, and he flashes out of the way, over to the other side of the fucking pool. I cross my arms over my chest. Tricky bastard.

"That's not fair, come back here and let me bite you! Then

sex you. Then bite you some more." Yeah, I notice when his eyes ink over again. Fucking bullseye. He shall be my sex putty, and we shall make metaphorical Dawn babies with my absent womb.

"Fucking hell, I'll be right back."

And then my Dawn God is gone, poof, just like that, and I have nowhere to channel all this overwhelming tension that's making my fluids leak. Where's a tap when you need one.

I run my finger along my lip, then dip that finger into my mouth, tasting the man who just devoured my mouth and told me he loves my inner beast. Fuck. I almost spontaneously orgasm on the spot.

Actually ...

I drop that same hand down my body, paying particular attention to my nipples through the soft fabric masking them, rubbing and tweaking them just the way I like it as my other hand dips under the hem of my shift, sliding my underwear to the side.

I'm still a little tender, but my vagina's come back to life with a vengeance, and I have the memory of my sexy Dawn God attempting to devour me whole to keep her satiated.

I lean back against the edge of the pool, thrusting my hips out so I can gain better access as I run my fingers through my folds.

God, he tasted good. I need me another dose of that honey.

Paying special attention to my clit with my thumb, I slip my fingers inside and work myself just the way I like it when I'm on my own ... rhythmic and deep.

In, out, swirl, swirl. In, out, swirl, swirl.

The sounds I'm making are not feminine, but I don't care.

So ... fucking ... good.

I wish this was Aero's mouth ...

That just threw me over the edge. I scream out as my

body curls forward, my vagina purring her satisfaction by clamping so hard around my fingers that I'm actually afraid I might fucking lose them up there.

I don't, thankfully, and when I open my eyes to see Aero and Drake watching me from the stairway island in the centre of the pool, I'm not even mad.

"Are you going to let me bite you now?" I ask Aero, who takes a sharp step forward before Drake throws an arm out to stop him, grabbing him tightly around the shoulder.

He's covered in dirt. Has he *actually* been ploughing fucking fields with Sol?

"You're coming with me, babe."

CHAPTER ELEVEN

"I'm not sure what I did wrong." I'm pouting like one of those females in Kal's harem. I don't care, because Aero wouldn't let me bite him.

Double pout.

"Nothing, babe," says Drake, coming at me with a cute little spatula. "Now poke your tongue out."

"Bossy today, aren't you?" But I do as he says, because I'm feeling malleable right now. He dabs some funky tasting green paste onto it and I try not to gag.

"I'm always bossy. But I'm the sexy kind of bossy. Not like Sol, who's just the bossy kind of bossy."

I think Sol's sexy too, but I don't say that aloud, because I'm pretty sure Sol and Drake have some kind of alpha male battle going on between them that's probably eons old.

"Do you want to talk to me about it yet?" Drake asks with a perfectly arched brow, and I know he's not talking about me wanting to gnaw Aero's arm off.

I shake my head. They shouldn't be trying to fix something that's already broken.

His lips purse. "Leave your tongue out until it goes numb,

then I'll wash the paste off and you should start to feel normal again. We might have to repeat the process, depending on how quickly the venom works its way out of your system."

Right. Lovely.

"I heal quickly." It sounds funny with my tongue hanging out.

"I've noticed. Even so I still want you to stay in bed for at least another day. Your body's still a bit fucked up, babe."

Drake, always so tactical with his words. "I love your pillow talk."

Tongue still out, I look around the room from my vantage point in the middle of the super comfortable, fuck-ten-people-at-once-bed I'm currently languishing in. The room appears to be carved into the side of a sandstone mountain, because I can see another mountain scape through my wide-open window, with windows, doors and balconies carved into it.

Everything is clean, simple lines with plush soft furnishings, and no decoration aside from the odd potted fig tree and climbing vine snaking up the sides of the walls.

"I'll show you around the rest of the place tomorrow."

"With Aero?"

"No, you're on an Aero ban. No Aero for you."

"I only need a little bit of him. Preferably his neck, but I'm happy with his bicep. Fuck, I'll even take his foot if that's all there is on offer. I'm not usually a foot person but I'll make exceptions."

"What was that?" he asks, cocking a brow.

Ugh. It's so fucking hard talking with your tongue hanging out of your mouth.

"What do you feel like for lunch? You've lost a lot of weight."

I wave my hand dismissively. "I'm not hungry."

"Like fuck. I'll get you some soup."

Lovely, that'll probably look fantastic coming back up. Like a fucking murder scene. I just smile around my tongue and nod like a good little patient.

I expect him to ring the gold bell on the wall, but he doesn't. "I'll be right back. Ignore the baby drako if you get a visit. Unlikely—the little fucker's not too fond of strangers and likes personal space, but I thought I'd better mention it."

"What the fuck?"

"You'll be right. Drakos' don't usually throw flames unless they're provoked."

"Hang on a minute ..."

"Keep your tongue out!" Drake winks, shutting the door behind him.

My Gods are so disobedient.

I have about three minutes to mull over the mental vision of the deep fissures between Aero's abdominals in perfect, peaceful bliss before I hear something flapping about outside my window. Well, Drake's window. I guess these are all his windows.

A tiny, gold baby drako alights on the sill, and appears to be contemplating whether or not it should enter through the wide-open window. It's cute as fuck, but those things breathe fire and have claws like daggers, even if it is only the size of a small dog.

I squirm as far as I can under the covers without licking the perfectly white sheets with my green tongue. I wish Drake had wiped this shit off before he left, my tongue has no sensation left whatsoever and I'm worried it might actually fall off.

The little fucker's fast—he's suddenly sitting on the edge of the bed, sniffing at me like I'm his next goddamn barbecue Lesser Fae feast.

I'm going to skin Drake alive if this thing fries me. That's another one of my worst nightmares … mainly because mum once told me it was a drako that fried the skin from her body. Hard to forget that shit, especially when your brain is an immaculate filing system that never runs out of storage space.

"Easy little guy …"

He cocks his head to the side, probably because I sound strangled with my tongue hanging out—a good meal target. He prowls up the bed towards me, sniffing the air as he does.

Motherfucker.

I try to pull my legs closer to my body, right before the thing fucking pounces, landing on my chest and forcing the air out of my lungs. He's lucky he's light because I'm pretty sure that could've re-fractured my rib if he weighed any more.

I'm lying as still as a motherfucking statue while he sniffs me all over; even pushing the covers down to my feet and smelling my toes, then back up again to my face, where he proceeds to lick the green shit from my tongue; probably enjoying the seasoning before he feasts on my fried flesh.

But then he stops, shakes himself all over like I've seen wet dogs do in the city after they roll in street sewage, and flops onto my stomach, fanning his gorgeous glistening wings down either side of him so they're half on me, half on the bed either side of me, and goes to fucking sleep.

I don't move, barely even breathe, trying not to spook the little fucker.

After what feels like a goddamn hour later, but is likely more like ten minutes, Drake backs through the door, food tray in hand, looking positively delectable in a sexy chef apron. "Sorry, had to whip some up from scratch, I wanted it to be fresh. Also, I think the herb salve needed some extra time to work because you were high as a fucking ki—"

"Yeah, so this happened," I whisper, pointing at the drako.

Drake drops the tray and stands there, eyes unblinking, mouth open as the soup spills across the floor.

I raise my eyebrows. "Likes his own personal space, huh?"

Drake got me more soup after he stood there like a statue for a few minutes longer. Eventually he got over his shock. He also cleaned up the mess himself, even though the pretty blonde maid with sex in her eyes offered to help several times too many. My inner greedy whore got her hackles up and I almost had to gag the bitch.

"You didn't swallow the green stuff, did you?" He's investigating my tongue at close range.

"Of course not." I gesture to the baby drako sleeping soundly on my belly. "He licked it off me."

Drake laughs. "*He*, is a *she*. And I've never seen her get so close to someone else before."

"Oh, okay. Well, maybe she likes females?"

He shakes his head and pops another mouthful of delicious soup in my mouth. Not going to lie, I'm moaning a little. Man knows how to cook. "She has plenty of exposure to women, she's just never taken to another person before."

I nearly snort the soup out of my nose holes. "Right. Thanks for clearing that up for me."

He shrugs, looking too fucking pleased with himself. "I've been around for a very long time, Dell. A man can get lonely."

"Is that why you got a baby drako? A little mini Drake to roam the skies with … or do you have plenty of them, too?" I don't know why but my voice sounds bitter. I reach over and stroke the drako's head, eliciting a purr as I scratch between her pretty, glimmering scales—perfect little reflective surfaces all over her pipsqueak body.

"No children. I've always been careful not to mate. I don't

want to spend eternity tied to a woman I'm only going to find interesting for a few minutes."

This time I do fucking choke. "Holy fucking sex machine! Tell me the truth, why don't you ..."

"I'm all about transparency. I've had plenty of sexual partners, all of them willing—just so we're clear."

"No more than me, I bet." Sexual partners, that is—not *willing* sexual experiences.

He's frowning at me now, though his expression is soft. "Dell ..."

I shrug, well, as much as I can with a sleeping, fire breathing creature sprawled across me. I don't want to give the little fucker a fright and lose an eyebrow. Or a face. "It's what we're both thinking."

He shakes his head, golden curls doing a dance of their own. "You're wrong, I'm not thinking it. I'm thinking about how beautiful you look cradling my baby drako."

Fuck.

My vagina just perked her little ears up.

I look down at the drako and my heart aches for my uterus that died long ago. I bet she would've been real fun to converse with. She probably would've mellowed out my vagina significantly, instead Little Ginny is all raunch and no mature alter ego.

"What's her name?" My voice sounds husky, nothing like Drake's but enough to give away the fact that I just got a healthy dose of arousal.

Drake's smiling as he runs his hand down her spine, causing the rumbling purr to thicken.

"Sap. She likes to lick it from the trees, probably why she ate your tongue salve; it has some in it. I rescued her—her parents were shot down by legionnaires. Though she looks small she's actually about fifteen. They grow slowly, and she won't reach full maturity until she's over five hundred years old."

I try not to look shocked, likely fail. Drake has his hands full with a girl who's probably going to be trapped in her teenage years for a good couple of centuries.

"Why did you keep her? Why not find her a new home with her kind?"

"I like having something to nurture and care for."

Fucking hell. Drake the controlling bastard who likes to fuck a lot just knocked my expectations right out of the water. I realise I'm staring at him like he has penises for arms.

"I think you might be a good man."

He smiles so wide I need to look away. I know I've said it before, but nobody should look that fucking perfect.

Red feathers. So many red feathers.

They're everywhere ... I'm drowning in them.

I fucking hate red feathers.

I swat my hand about, only causing them to converge further; into my hair, my ears ... I choke and pull one from my fucking throat.

They're scraping at my eyes, assaulting me in places that are far too exposed. I can't get away from them ... I can't fucking escape them.

My beast wants a go. This is her domain and she's revelling in it. She wants to eat these fuckers for breakfast. But I'm shaking too much, my whole-body jolting ...

I realise the feathers aren't red at all, they're a different colour entirely ...

"Dell ... Dell wake up. It's a nightmare, wake the fuck up, goddammit!"

I gasp, eyes snapping open. Where the hell am I?

Hidden under a canopy of gold fucking wings, that's where I am. I barely even see the half-naked Dusk God hovering over me, straddling me, cradling my face in one hand.

"Calm down ... It's night time. You've been sleeping. You're safe."

I'm not.

I never have been.

I know his feathers are gold, I can see they're fucking gold, but something's telling me they're not gold at all.

Is he about to throw me against the dresser over there?

Is he about to stick one of his feathers so far up my lady bits that I need someone else to pull it out for me?

Is he about to ...

I close my eyes, shaking my head.

I'm still dreaming, I must be still dreaming. I can't get enough breath and I've lost control of my body ... Kroe finally fucking broke me, for good.

A warmth blooms between my legs, awakening my petrified fucking vagina. I groan as the wave rolls in, caressing me in places I didn't even know existed, before receding.

Drake takes my wrists and pins them above my head. My eyes fly open again.

He's no longer looking at me like I'm some broken fairytale, instead he's looking at me like I'm something to fucking conquer. Something to gain *control* of.

I struggle against the vice-like grip he has on my hands, gritting my teeth as I fight him for purchase beneath that canopy of shimmering feathers ... representing the power he wields over me. His muscles roll and tense in the struggle to hold me at bay.

"Let go!" Screaming has never worked for me in the past, I'm not sure why I think it will now. I try to kick out, but my legs are pinned beneath his, his body hovering above mine in a way that's all too familiar.

Warmth surges between my legs again, thick and tantalising, like a breath tickling me in just the right spots. My back arches—I grit my teeth and renew my struggle. "What are you doing?" My breath is heady, rasped ... my mind scrambling for purchase.

He growls, a deep possessive sound that rumbles right through me. "Stop fighting me Dell. I'm not going to touch you. I'm not going to hurt you. You need to see that not everyone wants to fucking *take* from you."

Another wave of pleasure practically bruises me, the force two-fold ...

Holy fucking twat tingler ... why the hell am I fighting again? I close my eyes and groan like the animal I am, the scent of my slick inner thighs infusing the air about us.

"Sweet fucking Dusk God ..."

Another wave and I'm moaning ... my vagina's never had this sort of attention before, and he's not even touching me.

"Drake," he growls. "Use it, Dell. Say my name the next time you scream from my pleasure." His voice is all gravel and command, turning my body to putty as he plays my vagina like a fucking fiddle.

Another wave hits and I just can't help it. I scream his name so fucking loudly my voice cracks.

"Open your eyes. I want you to look me in the eye when you come for me."

I oblige, because there's no room for movement in his tone. It's nothing magical, nothing spectacular, just pure, undiluted confidence. He owns what he wants, and he takes fucking charge of it.

His eyes are hooded, exotic and carnal as he lets go of my hands. "Good girl. I've let go but I want you to keep them there, do you understand?"

I nod, stealing a glimpse of his wings and gulping back the rising emotion.

He takes my chin in his hand, holding it hostage as he bares his canines in my face. "Don't look at them, look at me. They're not important. I am. What I'm doing to your body. Can you feel it?"

I nod, trying to be a good girl and keep my eyes open.

He swallows, adam's apple bobbing. The sane part of me wants to lick it all over, maybe even graze my teeth along it …

Another wave, but this time it bites at me … like a tender niggle right across my clit. "Drake …"

He smiles, teeth flashing sinister. "Do you like that?"

In response I grind against thin air, struggling to keep my hands above my fucking head, because I want more friction. *Need* more friction.

Another wave, coupled with that same biting pleasure across the most sensitive parts of me, and I can't fucking take it anymore. My hand shifts to my torso, on a beeline for my clit …

He growls and the pleasure fucking *stops*.

I'm not embarrassed to say I'm whimpering. My vagina's shedding enough tears to drown a city.

"Put it back." His eyes are piercing, tone abrupt, crumbling my resolve.

Bloody hell.

Pouting, I do as he asks.

"Good girl."

Another wave washes over me, the sensation so fucking good it's agonising.

"Drake … touch me!" My back is arching so high I almost manage to rub my party pie against his *very* obvious erection. But he dances his hips just out of reach every. Fucking. Time.

"No. I've seen you pleasure yourself, but you don't know

how good it can actually be ... because you've never been treated the way you fucking *deserve* to be treated."

Well then ...

Another wave hits and my whole body curls off the bed. "Holy fucking ... fuck, I need you inside me, please ..." I've never needed anything so goddamn much before.

He shakes his head. "No, you don't need me. You don't need anyone. *You* are in control of your body. You just have to *let go*."

The next wave takes me where I've never before been. Body slick with sweat, I ride that fucking wave like the beast I am, as Drake devours me with his gaze, urging me over the precipice and into a pit of undulating pleasure so fierce I'm surprised my whole body doesn't collapse into itself, while I scream his name over and over.

The comedown leaves me with droopy lids, and something inside me that was broken before suddenly doesn't feel quite so ...

He throws me a heart shattering smile. "Good girl."

Yeah, I deserve a gold vagina star for that one—I hope he pins it to my chest. I'll call it my orgasm star. Don't underestimate the power of a good fucking orgasm, I guess.

He lays down next to me, one wing draped over my body possessively, a wing that now doesn't look quite so frightening.

I can feel Drake's gaze on me. "You can touch them."

I'm not sure I want to. But then, maybe I do ...

They're gold. *Gold.*

Let go, Dell.

Let. Go.

I reach out, hand trembling as I run my fingers through those glistening, golden feathers, bathed in light from the fire dancing in the hearth.

He lets out a deep, rumbling groan—eyes closed, features content. "Do it again."

I take a peek at his throbbing erection, standing loud and proud, pushed up against his linen pants that hide fucking nothing. I concede my own suspicions about giant penis number two. At least this God can give me an orgasm with his mind …

I pet my man-bird, studying his face as his brows knit and he chews his lower lip.

"Fuck." He closes his eyes. "It feels so good when you do that."

I do it again, just so I can store the image of his pleasure for when I'm alone, practising achieving the sensations he just roused in my previously under-appreciated vagina. Bitch has been living under a rock and she didn't even realise it.

She's screaming at me that we can't be without this man's magic orgasms again, ever, but I have her pinned against a wall, giving her a fucking pep talk—because this man goes through women like we went through cock at the whore house, bitch. We're just another plaything, don't get attached.

Too late … if I let her have free rein, she'd be clamped onto his leg, dry humping the godly bastard. He'd probably have to pry the bitch off.

"Do you ever just get a bunch of people together and make them all randy? Forge a giant orgy then sit back and enjoy your masterpiece like the fucking artist you are?" Because I would. Every opportunity I got I'd be forging orgies. I'd go down in history as a great and mighty being, the 'Bringer of Vaginal Happiness'. Everyone would be so fucking liberated.

He laughs from his belly and the smile meets his eyes. "I've done it before, when I had power to splurge."

Oh, right. With everything that's been going on I almost forgot they're running out …

"Why haven't you used your wish on me yet?"

All happiness disappears as he studies me in earnest. I've stopped playing bird whisperer, keeping my petting hands to myself.

He shrugs. "There's nothing I want from you."

I try to hold back my laugh and it comes out as a snort. "Yeah, that's not what a girl wants to hear when you just gave her a ground-breaking orgasm with your mind."

"No, bad fucking timing right there," he says, smiling.

"Seriously though Drake, just get it over with. I don't fit, you all need the power boost, I don't understand why you won't just do it."

He shakes his head. "I don't want to do it yet. I want to give to you, not take from you."

"Orgasms?" My whore vagina made me say it.

"Those, too, but more than that. I just want to be close to you. I know the other guys feel it too, which is fucking annoying because I don't like to share. It's not my thing. I nearly tore Aero's balls off when I heard he'd bitten your fucking tongue."

"I made him do that, it was entirely my fault."

He runs his finger along the base of my throat, then back again, and I can hardly breathe because it's sending tingles all the way to my nether regions. "I want *my* venom running through those veins of yours. Just mine. With you, I have no control, and it's stewing me up in ways you wouldn't understand."

"Talking about stewing …" Yeah, I need to vomit. My timings fucking impeccable, anyone would think I had an aversion to deep and meaningful conversations that elicit actual emotions.

Holding my hand over my mouth, I push my way out from beneath that giant wing and hurtle towards the washroom, slamming the door behind me and throwing myself at the toilet, where I shoot my ruby stomach jizz all over the goddamn porcelain.

Fucking hell, it's getting worse.

I hear some sort of commotion outside the bathroom, but I'm too busy hurling my guts up to take much notice.

"Get the fuck out of here, you know the risk!" Drake's pissed at someone.

"You need to go in there, now."

What the fuck is *Aero* doing here? Has he come to let me gnaw on his bicep finally?

"She's hiding something from us!"

Ohhhhhh shiiiiiit.

The door handle begins to turn ...

"Fuck off! Give a girl some privacy for shit sake!" I hurl some more, and I'm flushing the chain at the same time, leaving the water only slightly pink looking.

The door opens, but I don't have the energy to actually fight a fucking Sun God. "Ugh ..." I lay down on the cool, hard floor so I can gather myself, because I'm a trembling mess. And I'm tired from my orgasm. Really, I just want to go back to sleep.

Maybe after another orgasm ...

Strong arms scoop me up, lifting me off the ground. "You can fuck off now, Aero. I've got her." Drake carries me through to the bedroom where Aero is standing, half naked, looking ripe for the taking. I like my Dawn God rare, even if I am laying like a limp dick and quivering like a virgin at an orgy.

"I'm not going anywhere, but she needs another dose. Her metabolism has burnt it off already but her blood still has traces of my venom."

"There's no way you're putting that green shit on my tongue right now. Sorry."

They look at me blankly for a moment, then back at each other.

"Then take a spare fucking bedroom, otherwise she'll probably bite you in her sleep."

"Valid point," Aero grumbles, turning for the door.

Drake lowers me to the bed. Sap—back from her little night time flying adventure, crawls forward and nestles herself against my side.

Aero pauses, half out the door, turning back to look at me with a crinkled brow, that somehow manages to make him look even more bite worthy. His arse also looks really fucking tight in those pants.

"I know I just vomited and all, but I'm not against biting your bum right now if you're up for it?"

He doesn't even smile. Wow, someone's channelling their inner fun sponge again.

"Your drako likes her …"

Drake nods as he tucks me in meticulously. His wings are still out and taking up a lot of fucking space if you ask me. "Can't get enough of her. I had to throw her outside so Dell could get some sleep earlier."

They share a look that lasts for a few long seconds; they're purposely leaving me out of a conversation! Motherfuckers. And I'm too sleepy to argue.

"Tomorrow," says Aero, heading for the door. "No more fucking orgasms, arsehole." He slips out the door, slamming it shut behind him.

"Tomorrow what?" I ask, trying to mask the sound of my vagina's hysterical wails. I can have orgasms if I want to have fucking orgasms …

"Nothing, babe. Go to sleep."

"Mhm. Bite me."

Lights out.

CHAPTER TWELVE

I wake with Drake sleeping soundly next to me, looking all godly and perfect. Even his eyelashes are like spun gold. I'm tempted to run my finger along that square jawline, then up to the freckle high on his cheekbone that's practically *begging* to be licked.

"Like what you see, babe?"

Ahh …

I close my eyes and pretend to be asleep.

"Nice try, I felt you watching me. I also felt your arousal."

Shit almighty, he's also a fucking sex detector. I crack an eye open. "How can you *feel* someone's arousal?"

He stretches his arms above his head and I repress the urge to grind my vagina all over him. Fuck, is she rubbing off on me? She's so vulgar!

"It's part of my gift. I can perceive sensory stimulation." He pushes out his wings, stretching the muscles and taking up half the room.

"I was just admiring your freckle. It's a nice freckle." I don't tell him I want to *lick* said freckle, because I think it may come across a little creepy.

"I like yours too."

I blush … he means the one by my fucking bellybutton. I thought I was the only one who knew it was there … convenient time for a toilet break?

Clearing my throat and dodging a wing, I edge out of bed, doing my best not to disturb Sap who's still sleeping.

"Are you going to the toilet?"

I turn to see Drake sitting on the edge of the bed, looking conniving as fuck. "Yes, I am. Want to join me? I didn't know you were into that, but hey …"

He laughs, full and hearty. "I'm not, I just need you to piss in a jar for me."

What.

The.

Fuck.

I take a step backwards, then another, and the fucker's tensing like he's ready to pounce.

"*Why?*"

"I just need you to."

Yeah. Nah.

"I want many things in life, Drake, doesn't mean I'm going to get them. Unfortunately for you, same rules apply." I turn and run for the bathroom, but he's right there, barring the door before I can close it behind me, holding out a glass fucking jar.

"I'm not asking, I'm telling."

I look down at the jar in his hand. "You can shove that up your arse for all I care, I'm not peeing in a fucking jar."

"You think you can overpower a God, babe?" He looks bloody wicked, and a little amused.

I tap my foot on the ground. I really need to pee.

Growling, baring my canines at the bastard, I storm out of the bathroom. "Where's the kitchen? I'm hungry."

He folds his arms over his chest and sighs. "All right, I'll play. You're going to have to piss some time though, and when you finally explode, I'll be right there, between your legs, holding the fucking jar if I have to."

I stomp out of the room. I'll find the kitchen on my own.

Half an hour later I'm still wandering aimlessly along well-lit tunnels carved deep into the mountain, natural and raw. I consider how it's the complete opposite to the Day castle, that's all sparkles and glam. No wonder Sol and Drake don't get on, they're polar opposites who both have alpha streaks and one singular, cataclysmic similarity; they both like to be in control.

Recipe for fucking disaster if you ask me. I'm surprised they haven't killed each other already.

Speaking of Sol, I hope he comes to visit me soon—I have some serious grovelling to do.

"Need help finding food, babe?" Drake drawls from behind me. "Or a toilet?"

Wanker.

I peer through an arched doorway that's got to be ten times taller than me, and into a sprawling throne room, gasping at its splendour.

Intricate designs carved into the colossal walls and columns lining the space appear to tell a story, perhaps of things past, and happenings yet to come. The room must be big enough to fit a couple thousand people at least, the vast floor buffed to a high gleam, sending my eye skimming over the surface to that gold fucking throne perched on the ornate dais at the back of the hall … holy shit. That's one shiny, big boy chair.

"I'm sure I'll find it eventually," I mumble, jiggling.

Fucking bladder.

"Want to go in there?"

I jump so high I damn near piss myself because the bastard's suddenly right at my ear, so close that my arm hairs are reaching out to stroke him. I turn around and attempt to flatten him with a glare, but he just laughs.

"No. Thank you."

I should probably try and be polite to him now that I've seen his monolith fucking throne room. The guy's obviously a big deal around here—don't want to be seen disrespecting the man.

He steps further into my personal space, which has my vagina reaching her little arms out to grab him. Traitor. She's obviously not deterred by the fact that he wants to hoard my piss.

"What if I want you to," he purrs. "What if I want to take you to that throne, sit you on my lap, spread your legs and fucking *worship* you until you cum all over my fingers."

Fucking gulp. His nostrils flare ... my cheeks heat.

"You're not playing fair ..."

The fucker smirks, casually shrugging a shoulder. "Baby, I never play fair."

"Are you just trying to get me to squirt everywhere so you can bottle it up?"

The corner of his lip curls ever so slightly. "You said it, not me."

Bastard. I turn around and storm off, but a large hand wraps around my arm, halting me on the spot. "Wrong way." Drake hurtles us into the Bright so swiftly I almost vomit my empty guts up, landing us at a table laden with food.

I stare at the excessive feast before us, hoping we're not expected to eat all that on our own ...

Drake tugs a chair out for me at the head of the table, signalling for me to lower my wiggly arse onto the seat. Which I do. *Only* because it means I can tuck my leg under and try to block the golden gates with the heel of my foot.

Drake takes a seat along the side, close to me but leaving the seat at the other head free.

The large room overlooks the mountain scape—lush, fertile land with a chasm running between the middle of the two peaks, like a ying and yang mountain island in the middle of the ocean.

I look back to the table, and frown. "Do we *need* all this food? Seems a bit excessive if you ask me."

Bacon, eggs, pastries, cheeses, grapes ... even fucking caviar, which I was once 'treated' to in Kroe's chambers. The thought of eating that at this time of the morning makes me want to hurl all over the table.

Aero strolls in wearing his metal god gear I'd hoped to one day peel off him myself, looking all casual and fucking cool, running his gaze over me and scenting the air before he sits down at the other head of the table.

I don't want to bite him as much anymore, and it's nice to feel like I'm not going to jump the guy and start gnawing on his arse. Though, I still like the thought of sinking my teeth into his neck ...

"We eat a fuck tonne," Drake says, filling his plate. His wings are still out, spread wide and resting behind him.

Right, better get to it then. I pour myself a glass of water and pluck a small stem of grapes off the overwhelming pile before me.

Fuck, I need to piss. I wiggle my hips a little, curling my foot beneath me further. Looking up, I catch Aero watching me over the top of a glass of juice.

"*What?*"

He shakes his head, then looks across to Drake. "This is going to be harder than we thought."

"I'm aware of that, Dawn. I haven't wanted Sol's company before in my very long existence, but right now, he would be very fucking handy."

"Are you guys talking about me peeing in a jar?"

They look at each other, then back to me, nodding.

Sexy sickos.

I roll my eyes and take a sip of water. "Take your pee fantasies elsewhere. Not judging, it's just not my thing."

Drake looks at me like he's staring down the blade of a sword. "I'll follow you around with that jar all day if I have to. Though by the looks of things, that won't be necessary."

Yeah, okay, so I'm doing a lot of squirming and my fucking foot's jammed hard against my pee hole, trying to plug the fucker.

I take another sip of water then realise it's only going to make the pee situation worse. Groaning, I slam the glass down on the table, unplug my pee hole, stand and start pacing the room.

Drake shifts his wings, looking like he's prepared to pounce at the drop of a golden droplet.

"Why the fuck do you need my pee, anyway?"

Aero clears his throat and I eye him like I have a score to settle. Because I do. First, he kissed me into oblivion, then he wouldn't let me chew on his bicep, and now he wants a jar of my pee? I don't like the direction our relationship's going. A steady fucking decline, that's what it is.

"Urinology."

Fuck no.

What I want to do is throw myself out that wide open window, into the chasm of water down there where I can pee to my heart's content without a Sun God holding a fucking jar between my legs.

Aero flashes before the windows, thwarting my escape plan, wings spreading wide and eliciting a low hiss from Drake; who's now standing, eyeing Aero up and down like they're in some sort of gladiator match where they're expected to fight to the death. His wings are spread far and wide too. He looks positively ruthless and, not going to lie, fucking hot.

I feel like I'm trapped in the middle of something I really don't understand.

"So, you want to taste my piss?" I say, trying to ignore all the tension in the room and the overwhelming scent of male dominance.

"This is my kingdom, fucker. Put them away." Drake's eyes are beginning to ink over ... yeah, so are Aero's.

"You've never been anal about this before, arsehole. Now's not the time!"

Drake fucking *hisses* at him, and it's so goddamn feral it makes me jump. Are they about to have a territory battle because Aero brought his wings out in Drake's dining room? Fucking hell, these Gods need a full-time babysitter. I'm not sure I'm up to the challenge.

Aero hisses back and it occurs to me that these guys should know better than to beef over land at such a ripe old age. They might have a coronary and die.

I realise Drake's readying his muscles to pounce and I throw my hands up in fucking defeat. "I'll pee in your motherfucking jar, okay! Just put the fucking wings away and calm the fuck down. Both of you."

I snatch the jar, conveniently placed at my end of the table and storm off in search of a bathroom.

"I swear to God, if *either* of you drink my pee you will *not* live to tell the tale!"

They didn't drink my pee. Instead, Aero flew that golden jar off to some uranology master, apparently. But if he comes back smelling like urine I'll never trust the fucker again.

Drake's showing me around the rooftop garden, which is

more like an exotic forest full of unique plants and flowers, while I ponder over how I'm going to convince him to give me another orgasm.

A flash almost knocks me to the ground, accompanied by a sound that makes me think the fucking sky is splitting in two. I shield my eyes from the brightness before it quickly fades away, leaving two dirty Sun Gods standing in front of us. A second flash brings Aero in, too.

My Dawn God's looking at me like he's confused, and Kal's wearing a guilty scowl that even the dirt he's smeared in can't hide. Sol's filthy too, muscles slick with sweat and clumps of mud and grass clinging to his clothes. Perhaps they've been ploughing *actual* fields and not *actual* vaginas after all ... huh.

Sol's looking at me like he wants to cut a bitch. Confused, I drop my gaze ...

He's holding my fucking box! And *not* the one that's been gagging for attention all morning.

Feeling the blood drain from my face, I spear my attention at Aero. "You fucking promised!"

"I didn't tell them where it was!" he says, looking hurt. "I buried it twenty feet underground in the fields in the Day Kingdom, then dug up the whole fucking field so nobody would notice. I did my best to hide it ... you should have worded the wish differently—I couldn't stop them!"

"I was under duress!"

Sol kneels, then opens the lid to my private fucking possessions. I'd be gouging out his eyes right now if Drake weren't holding me to him like I'm a feral fucking hostage. Then I remember Drake coming to collect me at the Dawn Kingdom ... covered in dirt.

The fucker knew they were looking for it. He was helping them ...

I groan, squirm, and try to pull away.

Looking murderous, Sol holds up a long, white feather. "What's this, Dell? Where the *fuck* did you get this from? Are you his fucking *spy?*"

I'm choking on my emotions, gagging on them. I don't realise I'm crying until a tear lands on my arm.

"Fuck you guys, fuck you all!" I hiss, and Drake finally lets me go. I stumble forward, spinning in a circle and looking them all in the eye, arsehole by arsehole. "I fucking hate you all."

I pick up my box, snatch the feather out of Sol's fucking hand and storm off down the stairs. "Don't fucking follow me, I never want to see *any* of you again!"

Wow, I have a real flair for theatrics. Fucking arseholes.

Suppress, Dell. *Suppress.*

I take hallway after hallway, down, never up. I need to go down as far as I can, then I might find a way out of this fucking place.

Hallway, stairs. Hallway, hallway, stairs. My surroundings become darker and cooler the further I go, clutching my box to my chest. The sound of rushing water intensifies with every flight.

Eventually I come to a doorway framed with thick foliage. I can hear the water flowing nearby. I hope there'll be a boat somewhere downstream for folk like me who can't fucking fly, though I doubt it. I might be making one myself. How hard can it be?

Maybe the tide will carry me straight to the East where I can live out the rest of my days as Dell the Orgasm Master. I'll hone the skills Drake taught me and spend the rest of my years teaching women how to play with themselves. Good plan, I'm a fucking genius.

It occurs to me I should have packed snacks for the road, but I'm not going back. Ever. Nosey bastards. I'll learn to fish with my teeth and hope I don't form a mating bond with any of the scaly little suckers while I'm at it.

I clamber over rocks and branches along the edge of the river; it's cold and I'm really wishing I'd packed a fucking bag with warm clothes. There's a lot to be said for pre-planning. The cold saps my energy faster than I would usually lose it.

Finding a little cave near the water that's half covered in moss, I nestle my way in there. It's cramped but it has a great view of the river and any potentially approaching Sun Gods. I wonder how I would fare in my own territory battle, because I wouldn't mind pitching a house here for a bit, while I build my boat and learn to catch fish with my teeth. Though I'd have to go up against Drake, and he's scary when he gets all dark eyed and territorial. Hmm, I don't like my chances.

I pop my box on a ledge, crack the lid open and reach inside.

A mini canine is the first thing to come out—I quickly find the other one. My baby teeth. They fucking fell out when I was twelve and I freaked out, so I kept them in case I found a way to plug them back in.

It's frightening when random shit happens to your body and you've got nobody to talk about it with, except the dark. My adult ones eventually grew in, but I couldn't bring myself to part with my little ones. They're so cute.

I lift out a smooth grey stone that fits perfectly in the palm of my hand. There's nothing particularly unusual about it; just your regular river rock, except that it's the exact hue of my mother's eyes. I've kissed that stone more times than I could count. I do so now, then place it gently to the side.

A red feather, the one that once found a nice, cosy home in my vagina. Fucker.

A white ribbon, my favourite. It was in my hair that day

... I run my fingers along the surface, enjoying the peaceful texture, pausing when I reach the tiny droplets of blood.

I breathe it in then pop it to the side.

A beautiful piece of amber, given to me by my mum—within it, a white moth suspended in time. It probably went in for a lick and ended up fucking dying. Poor little guy. It's been a constant reminder to keep my tongue to myself ... most of the time. But I love it, because it's beautiful and my mum gave it to me. I run my finger over the smooth edges then give it a sniff, before placing it to the side.

Next, a small, corked vial, no longer than the palm of my hand and filled with something brown—don't ask me what because I have no idea. I've opened the lid, but only a few times, because whatever the fuck's in there smells like Satan's shit left to rot for a millennia. I keep it because my mum gave it to me, and I love her, even if her gift does smell like rotten arsehole.

Finally, the pure white fucking feather. I frown at it then put it straight back in the box.

They should learn to keep their noses in their own fucking business, those Gods.

Shivering and feeling lightheaded, I pack all my bits away then close the lid on my past and curl into a little ball to preserve warmth, trying to ignore the nagging pain in my stomach that's been intensifying since this morning.

Groaning, I rock; partly to ease the pain, partly for comfort. My stomach cramps in agonising spasms, I convulse, gagging, barely make it to the water's edge where I vomit blood, causing what looks like a fucking murder scene to drift downstream. Sweating, I splash cold water on my face and stagger shakily to my feet.

The sound of crunching leaves catches my attention.

"Fuck off!" I yell, at whoever the hell thinks it's a good

idea to corner me right now. Don't they know I've got a history of biting men's penises off?

"I'm not here to put my penis in your mouth."

Aero. It wouldn't fucking fit in there anyway.

I crawl back into my cave and curl in a ball around my box. "This is *my* territory now, so fuck off. I told you I don't want to see you again."

"Your territory? That's a brazen statement considering you're in *my* kingdom."

Bastards. They never take me seriously.

"Fuck off Drake, you traitor. It's only a little cave, you won't even notice I'm here."

"I can't give you orgasms from such a large distance, babe."

My vagina sees his reasoning and nods her little head in agreeance, but I gag the bitch before she has a chance to speak.

"I don't need your fucking orgasms; I've got my own." I curl myself tighter.

"Just compel her out, you wanker!" That's Sol. Fucking lovely. I wasn't aware I sent out a group invitation.

"I'm not compelling her; she could be a spy."

"Fuck you, Sol! And to think I was going to apologise to you for being an arse. *You're* the arse. Go graze on some grass, or cunt, whichever you prefer. Doesn't fucking bother me."

It's a lie, of course. I was hoping he would graze on *my* cunt, but I've just pissed *that* idea up against the wall because he invaded my privacy and he thinks I'm a spy.

"I'll deal with this."

"No, Kal! You leave your emotional blackmail shit well the fuck away from me! Or else I'll castrate you in your sleep. You all know I'm capable of it so don't fucking try me!"

It goes silent. I let out a little sigh of relief and snuggle into myself further, utterly exhausted. Arguing with Sun Gods is hard work, I'm so outnumbered.

I can't believe that actually worked—I feel like a bear who just defended her cave.

A sleepy, hibernating bear…

Wait… "Motherfucker!"

Lights out.

CHAPTER THIRTEEN

What's worse than going to sleep in a cave feeling like death warmed up? Waking up in some random fucking house realising you *are* death warmed up, especially when you're surrounded by angry, solemn, stunned, or screaming Sun Gods who think they were invited to a stomach cancer pity party. Although apparently it's no longer just stomach cancer. I don't do anything by halves.

It hasn't been a shock to me—other girls at Kroe's get it. Though it's by no means been confirmed, my theory is that it's the 'mineral water' we're forced to drink every morning in replacement of a meal—the one that's supposed to be great for our health but also provides us with unnatural energy. It's got all sorts of strange shit in it. It doesn't take long for girls to start vomiting up blood. Some last longer than others, most die or disappear for other reasons before it becomes too serious.

Like I've said before, I'm surprised I didn't die years ago. It's about time my mortality caught up with me.

"She doesn't have cancer! Fucking heal her now!" Sol's

been yelling at the lady who tastes piss for a living since I woke up. He's real subtle. Such a gentleman.

"Stop yelling at the poor woman, she's probably really busy, okay? Plenty more piss to taste, let's just leave her to it."

Nobody even looks at me in my sick person's cot over here. Wankers.

"You can try and compel me to heal her all you like, Milord, but there's nothing there to heal. The girl is *dying*. By all means though, keep trying." She gives Sol a pointed glare before turning around and putting some elbow grease into her pestle and mortar she's grinding like a boss bitch.

I like this woman, she's got sass. Anyone who's got the guts to stand up to Sol is fine by me.

"But I will make her a tonic, which should take care of the nausea. Dying of starvation would be a really shit way to go."

I was wrong, I don't like this woman at all. I fucking *love* her.

I ignore the chest growl Sol uses to show us all his alpha-male manliness. I'm not even sure why he gives a shit about me dying—he's made it pretty clear lately how little he thinks of me.

I look over at Aero, who's been struggling to keep his eyes from inking over since I woke in this quaint little healer's hut, which smells like a herb garden had sex with some highly illicit drugs. He snaps his gaze to me then shakes his head, crunching his lids shut and continuing to pace like a caged bull.

His wings keep trying to pop out, like two back penises rising to the occasion. Not that I have a dirty mind or anything, but now it's been confirmed I'm actually dying, I feel like my vagina deserves to have a little free rein. Kind of a last hurrah. Maybe I'll let her try his massive penis out after all—death by Dawn God cock wouldn't be such a bad way to go…

Oops, there he goes, storming out the front door. A couple of flaps of his wings and he's gone.

Something tells me these guys aren't used to losing people, I guess that's the catch when you spend your life around immortals, rather than the mortal ones.

We're fragile, but most of the time we have a lifetime to get used to that.

Drake's curled over in a chair, face in his hands. I wonder if it's an inappropriate time to ask for an orgasm? Yeah, probably. But I *do* feel like I need to make the most of this vagina while I still have enough faculties left to enjoy it…

The round woman with lots of freckles and a kind face hands me a small cup of tonic and motions for me to throw it back, I'm guessing in one hit? So I shoot it back like a boss and try to give her an encouraging smile, almost vomiting the foul tasting stuff back up when she turns to shuffle back towards her work bench.

Pretty sure this isn't the effect it's supposed to have… but hey, I'm no expert.

Kal's looking out the window, one hand in his fuck-me trousers that cling to his arse like a candy wrapper and the other is grasping his face that has a two-day old shadow. I thought I saw a tear rolling down his cheek before, but then I quickly averted my gaze. I don't know how to deal with that shit.

"How long?" I'm so glad Sol's finally stopped yelling at the poor woman for doing her job.

She looks at me over her shoulder, then back to Sol before answering in a soft tone that she probably thinks my Lesser ears can't hear. "Weeks, days… I'm surprised she's still alive. I didn't even have to taste her urine to know what's going on."

Cue feral Fae growling and hissing from High Fae Sun God pity squad. Aero lands by the door, tucks his wings in and storms the place, looking like he wants to reign some godly hell on the poor woman.

Overall, the mood is sombre as fuck, and I've had enough.

"Right," I say, pushing my covers back. "It's been fun and all, but I only have a few days left to live and I don't want to spend them in here, marinating in my own pity party." I stand up and nobody tries to stop me, thankfully, because I'm not against using the 'dying girl card'. Low, even for me.

I storm out of the hut like a badass, carrying my box and wearing nothing but a light linen shift, though it's not really storming because I'm super lightheaded and weak. But yeah, very quickly I realise I have no idea where the fuck we are, except that it's high on a hill overlooking the ocean with nothing to see forever but that tiny island over there with two palm trees.

"Typical," I mutter, realising why none of them felt it was necessary to chase me out of the hut. Where the fuck could I run to anyway?

I start down the hill towards the ocean, because it would be nice to feel the sand between my toes before I die. But once I reach the beach, I realise I don't want to stop, and put my box on a tall rock where it's nice and safe before heading straight for the water.

"Dell…"

Great. Kal probably thinks I can't swim because I spent my life fucking instead of learning the basics of life. But no, Mum taught me to swim when I was two. She loved the ocean. She told me it had saved her once … that it had saved me.

The tears take me by surprise, just like the temperature of the water. It's colder than I would've expected, but it's probably exactly what I need right now.

"For fuck's sake, Dell. Please, stop!"

That's not happening, because I don't just repel other people's emotional baggage, I also repel my own.

I dive beneath the waves, relishing in the freedom and vulnerability as I churn slowly through the water towards the small island that looks like a swell place to die. It's a slow process though, because my body's got a bit of cancer gnawing at its insides. But slow is the new badass and I don't intend to go down meekly. At least it gives me a chance to work the tears out of my system so I can pretend they never happened in the first place.

I'm vaguely aware that I'm being followed, but I do my best to ignore whoever was stupid enough to enter into shark infested waters to swim across a channel that's probably a breeding ground for fish. In short, I'm surprised when Kal and I drag ourselves out of the water and onto the small island.

I look over my shoulder at him. He's staring at me like I'm fucking insane. When he opens his mouth to say something, I beat him to it. "Let me guess, you're about to ask me if I have a death wish?"

Now he looks like he wants to murder me. Fuck, I'm on fire.

He's slick with the ocean and I know it's inappropriate to be thinking this right now, but he really *does* look like wet sex on a wet stick. Hot damn. His hair's dripping onto his face and his shirt's clinging to his body like a second skin. I need to take a step backwards before my vagina latches onto a limb and slowly devours him, because actually, that anti-nausea tonic really did the trick. I was *so* wrong to pre-judge the foul-tasting liquid.

"This isn't fucking funny, Dell." He takes a step towards me.

"I'm not laughing."

I can see the others launching off the shore over there;

gold, silver, and auburn wings gliding through the air towards us. I hope Drake's in an orgasm giving mood and that Aero's keen for his magic lips to become acquainted with my labia. I'm not sure what I want for my last meal, but my vagina's already put her requests in.

"Don't fool with me. Those waters are swarming with sharks! I had to convince them all they weren't fucking hungry just so you didn't become their dinner!"

Oops. Now that, I do feel bad about. A shit ton of wasted energy right there, and these guys are going to need all they have if they're going to survive this shit against the King.

I was supposed to be a leg up. I still can be …

The other three land behind me as I take a step towards Kal. "Use your wish."

"What? Are you fucking kidding me?" He's looking at me like I've got jizz on my face.

"Why would I joke about this shit right now? You need the power boost, I need it off my conscience; it's a win, win. Then I can go to my grave feeling like I've done my part."

There's some feral Fae growling going on behind me and I turn to see Sol pacing the island, Aero crouching while he kneads his palms into his eyes and Drake staring at me with his arms crossed over his chest.

I turn back to Kal. "I got you *laid* with my wish, the least you can do is fucking *use* yours."

He shakes his head, taking two steps towards me and ending up right in my face. "You have no fucking idea how we feel, do you? No fucking idea." He sidesteps me and storms over to that palm tree, dropping himself down next to it.

Man. Pity party has turned into pity island.

Fucking swell.

It gets better. And by better, I mean one of my gods' ferries an oversized hammock here to swing between the two palm trees. I plan to have many orgasms on it, just as soon as I have the energy to rouse my vagina from her comatose state.

As it is, I hardly have the energy to lift a finger right now. That swim took a lot out of me. At least I'm not aching from the inside out anymore, so on a 'feel good scale'—I'm not doing too bad considering I'm dying. But hey, it could be worse ... the view's to die for, I'm on an island with four fucking Gods and at least I'm not going to go out choking on a penis.

They take turns flashing in and out, never leaving me alone for a second, building a fire and bringing other supplies to make this a nice, cosy death island. I have to hand it to them, they're resourceful. One of them even brought my box over for me, which I've got tucked safely at the base of one of the palm trees I'm swinging from. Another brought a fucking chamber pot and built a three-way wall around it, with sticks and old palm leaves.

I'm still angry with them, but I don't want to die alone. And I lied, I don't hate them; they just tore open a wound that I've gone to great lengths to hide from, and it fucking stung. They have no idea the pain I've gone through trying to keep that door sealed firmly shut most of my life.

I'm torn out of my melancholy by the sight of a speckle of gold barrelling towards us across the sea. I make a half-assed attempt at perching myself up and shielding my eyes from the sun, so I can catch a clearer glimpse of ... what the hell *is* that?

"Is that Sap?" Kal sounds awed as all four of my Sun Gods peer into the distance, watching that gold speck get progressively bigger.

Drake nods. "The little fucker must've gotten bored. I

hope she didn't fry the hair off her babysitter to get away, like she did the last one ..."

"What?" I croak.

Drake frowns at me over his shoulder. "Go back to sleep, Dell. Your body needs the rest."

I roll my eyes. I'm feeling fine at the moment, actually. Not in pain at all. Overbearing bastard.

He takes a step forward, holding out his arms as Sap converges on the air space of my little pity island, though she flies straight past him and onto my dying chest.

"Oomph."

Her wings wrap around me and she licks my face with a tongue that smells suspiciously like fried sheep.

I smile at the little fucker. She seems to like me ...

All good, no big deal ... I'm definitely not crying. That's drako drool. Certainly not a mix of both. Fuck, this thing is really pulling on my flaccid heart strings. I wish she wasn't so goddamn adorable.

Drake's scratching the back of his head, making that bicep bulge and looking like a total fucking snack, but his eyes are telling a different story. Like he's a *sad* snack ...

I pat the pint sized fire breather's head and frown at my Dusk God. "Don't worry, you'll be her number one again real soon. I'm just fresh meat." She slathers my face with more licks. "Apparently really *tasty* meat ..."

And dying meat. Though I don't think it's the right time for another death joke just yet. Got to ease them in slowly, a bit like how I wish I'd been eased into anal.

I really hope the little fucker's not basting me for a good roasting.

Drake turns around and storms off to the other side of the island, plopping himself down by the water, his back to me.

"Is my ancient Dusk God sulking because he's jealous of a

dying girl cuddling his pet drako?"

"That's not what it's about at all, Dell." Aero stomps off, looking all dark and broody, then flops down next to Drake at the shore over there.

Cryptic bastards.

Sap snuggles closer into me, curling her tail up and rooting around until she's got a nice little Dell nook, before she burps and almost sets the fucking hammock alight—though Kal is quick to extinguish that shit—and goes to sleep.

She's warm, cute, and her scales only scratch me a little, so I don't mind snuggling her, but after a couple of hours of endless rumbling emanating from the sleeping pocket rocket, the last hour of which I've watched Sol stalk back and forth across the island like he's about to combust, Drake emerges from his sulk and plucks Sap up in a big Dusk embrace. She yawns then flops her head into the crook of his neck and goes straight back to sleep.

Fuck it.

Why does he have to look so fucking good cradling the sleeping baby fifteen-year-old drako when I'm on my death bed? Not to mention my absent uterus. So unfair.

Drake dishes me a sweet half smile that tells me he doesn't actually hate me for getting the first Sap cuddle afterall, and gently lays her down onto a pre-arranged, specifically crafted Sap nest, which is really just a hole in the ground he's packed full of blankets and hot rocks from the fire, but still, it's thoughtful as fuck.

Sol makes a beeline for me, on another soul-destroying mission from ground patrol. I ignore the bare feet, chiselled abs with a deep V leading to the linen pants hanging tantalisingly off his hips, making him look casual and tasty at the same time.

"Can I lay with you? I think we need to talk."

Well, knock me down with a fucking feather, I never thought Sol would be the one to initiate *this* conversation. I've been trying to work my way up to it, but I just couldn't quite get there. Plus, I was drako-sitting a pint-sized cutie.

"Sure, shuffle onto my death bed. There's room for two."

"Fucking hell, Del." But he obliges, and I do my best to move over. "Just let me do the work," and he does, lifting me then settling me back down onto his half naked body. Even my comatose vagina's purring in her sleep as he rests those massive arms around my body, making me feel fucking miniature. But also, pretty damn cosy and safe, even though I'm dying.

"I'm sorry ..." I say, keeping my eyes on the ocean. I can't look him in the eye right now. "I'm sorry I used my wish to force your hand. I know I fucked up."

He doesn't say anything, probably because he's just as uncomfortable in these types of situations as I am. I'm surprised we're getting anywhere at all, that we haven't tried to lop each other's heads off just yet.

Another death joke, I'm on fire right now.

Aero hisses from over there somewhere, but I ignore him. He's been stomping around for the past hour, battling against that dark side that keeps slipping in then out again.

"Truth is, I thought I went back to get my box. Turns out I actually went back to get my girls. If I had my chance over again there's nothing I would change, though perhaps I would've tried to achieve it without grating you up the wrong way."

It's a shit apology, but it's better than nothing. And it's an honest one.

The silence sits between us for a very long time, long enough for me to think that he's fallen asleep. Eventually I peek up at him and find him staring down at me like I'm some sort of fascinating conundrum.

"Have you been looking at me this entire time?"

He nods, saying nothing.

Finally, he clears his throat. "I'm sorry I invaded your privacy, and I'm sorry I called you a spy. I've had some time to think about it and I've realised the error of my ways; nobody could take the sort of shit you've been through and still work for the King."

Classic Sol. A well thought out, blunt, no theatrics apology that gets straight to the fucking point, but then also misses the point altogether because he's got a carrot stuck up his proverbial backside.

"Thanks. If I weren't dying, I'd probably still be mad at you, but at the same time, if I weren't dying, I doubt I would've apologised in the first place. So, we're as bad as each other."

I get a smile out of him for that one, probably because he knows I'm bang on the clitoris. I'm going to miss these moments, when Sol shocks me with tender little quirks that remind me he's not a total controlling, soul eating psychopath. It's the small things.

I look out across the water. "You need to use your wish, Sol."

He shakes his head. "I'm not taking anything from you."

Fucking hell, what's with these guys? I push myself up off his chest, even though my vagina's mourning the loss of his earthy scent and the bulge of his pectorals beneath my head. I try to remind her she hasn't got the energy to do anything about it anyway, overeager twat.

"Then what the fuck was this all for then? A waste of everyone's time? Just fucking take it!" Yeah, so that got everyone's attention. I can sense them watching, subtly shifting closer through the sand.

"I'm not doing this with you right now." He gets up, plops

me back into my swinging death bed, and storms off towards the water, leaving me hanging. Literally.

"Then when do you want to do it, Sol? Because I don't know if you've noticed but we're running out of time!" Ok, so I've gone into full blown bitch mode. The cuddle was nice while it lasted, but now we're back to trying to stab each other's eyes out. I want to feel like my life has been worth something, but that's swiftly slipping through my fingers like the aftermath of a successful hand-job.

"Why do you think that is, Dell?" I turn my attention on Aero, who's looking about ten shades deep into his dark alter ego and is prowling towards me like a panther sniffing out his prey. The sun has turned his perfect honey toned skin a deep shade of amber, and he's dappled with a light sheen of sweat.

I shake my head at the bastard. "Do you need me to spell it out for you? I'm dying! What's got your panties in a twist?"

He uses his wings that won't seem to fucking disappear, to throw himself through the air, landing right in-front of me and making me tumble back into the hammock as he gets all up in my funk, breath tickling my face.

"Exactly! You should've told us you were dying! You fucking *knew* you were dying, and you purposely hid it from me, going to the extent to keep it from your fucking thoughts!"

Eeek.

I have to concede he's got me there, I just didn't think much of it. I became acquainted with death at a very young age.

"So yes, I'm fucked off. Which is really fucking annoying because all I want to do is kiss you."

Shit, that got my breath all heady really fucking quickly. I tilt my face up to him and part my lips, because if I'm only going to live a few more days then why the hell not?

"Then fucking do it."

He moves forward so quickly I barely have the chance to catch my breath, but the kiss isn't gentle or sweet, it's punishing and rough.

Our lips clash and he growls into my mouth, raking his tongue along mine as our teeth clank together in feral vigour.

I let out a little moan. My vagina's well and truly roused, and even my beast has cracked open an eyelid for the first time in forever, which confuses the shit out of me. Plunging my hands into the hair on the back of his head, I crush his face into mine and elicit another growl from deep inside him. But the need within is becoming potent, my insides coiling with angst of a thirst screaming to be quenched.

It's my beast, I realise, screaming at me to set her loose.

He pulls back, just enough for us to catch a fevered breath, firmly cradling my face in his hands. "Let her at me …"

"She'll eat you up …"

"I don't fucking give a shit."

Holy fucking god testicles. I hope he's got some sort of penis insurance.

I let her at him.

She pounces like the animal she is, launching forward and curling our limbs around his body, tugging him closer and kneading our hands into his muscles as they coil with the strength he needs to keep us held up.

We're clinging to him like a fucking lioness, ready to devour this man. It's strange—all my beast has quirked her ears at before is the prospect of gaining revenge over the fucktards who've brutalised me over the years.

Sucking his lip into our mouth, running our tongue along it, we taste his own desire and tug back, using our other hand to pry his head to the side and expose his neck to us. My beast roams our eyes over all the canvas there, running our tongue over the tips of our canines as my beast contemplates where she's going to sink our teeth into this man.

He groans, sending her fucking rabid, launching toward the spot a couple of inches below his ear, just as someone fucking grabs me from behind and pries me off my tasty Dawn God.

We roar, my beast and I. Like, an actual fucking roar, as Sol and Kal step in front of me, chests heaving and doing nothing to hide their engorged man bits.

"I wasn't going to eat him, I just wanted a taste!"

Drake's not letting us go, damnit. He probably thinks we're going to chew Aero's cock off. That's not at all what we want to do, actually. My beast wants to lick and nurture that oversized tool of glory.

"Calm down, babe, calm down. Come back to the light …"

My beast coils away, whimpering, and I flop into Drake's arms. "What the fuck was that?" I don't think his question was directed at me, so I don't bother to answer.

Kal and Sol part. There's Aero, poised in a peculiar position that looks terribly uncomfortable. I narrow my eyes at Sol. "Are you compelling him?"

He shrugs. "Easier than throwing a bucket of ice water over his head to stem the flow of blood to his cock and return it to his fucking brain."

I roll my eyes, though it's an effort to do so because I'm sleepy all of a sudden. "Kal, if this is your doing, I'm *actually* going to castrate you this time."

He shakes his head, shifting closer and pushing a rogue curl from my eyes. "Not me, doll. Let go, your body's exhausted and you need the rest."

He's right. Being a feral sex deviant, hell bent on biting my sexy Fae Gods while my body's trying to die is hard work.

CHAPTER FOURTEEN

I wake to a swinging world. It feels late in the afternoon though not dusk yet.

I lift my head and realise I've managed to drool all over Drake's chest in my sleep. "Oops, sorry ..." my voice is groggy, like my head.

"Don't worry about it, I'm used to Sap drooling all over me. It's much more pleasant coming from you."

I've noticed how empty my little pity party island is. "Where've the others gone?"

"Sap went hunting for rodents."

Sure enough, there's the baby drako bouncing around over there on that island, throwing cute little flames and shit. I have to admit, she looks pretty harmless. I can't believe I thought she could melt me into a puddle when I first met her. Still ... I hope she doesn't set that medicine hut on fire ...

"And the others?" I ask, tearing my eyes away from all that flailing cuteness.

"Tending to some business. You've been asleep for almost an entire day. They shouldn't be too long." He runs his other hand through my hair, smoothing it down.

Almost a fucking day? That's probably why my vagina's pleading to me that it's her time to shine.

"Time for an orgasm?"

He shakes his head, frowning. "No, babe. I'm already expelling an excessive amount of energy to keep the pain at bay."

Huh?

Fucking hell ... these men.

That's why I haven't been in pain since I woke up in that pee-tasting hut over there. This is *not* okay.

I perch myself up, pushing his hands off me and ignoring his confused expression. "Drake, you need to make your wish. This is getting fucking ridiculous."

He nods, features smoothing, his gaze meeting mine with a deep intensity that almost makes me want to coil into my shell. "I agree, babe. It is getting ridiculous."

He puts his hand on the back of my head, pushing me down towards his chest and bringing both arms around my body, securing me tightly against him. Then he starts to glow, literally fucking glow, and it takes my dying brain a moment to realise he's initiating dusk.

I sink further into his body, lulled by the power surging out of this man beneath me. He pulls his lips in close to my ear, his breath tickling the sensitive skin there. "I wish for you to get better..."

A wave of heat rolls over my skin, before sputtering out like a spent candle.

His arms tighten. "I wish for you to get better!" He growls the words, kneading the hair at the back of my head.

The same wash of warmth swarms over me, heating me from the inside out before once again sputtering to nothing, even as I'm blinded by the light of the power flowing from Drake as he calls upon dusk, turning our surroundings golden.

"I wish for you to get *better*!" His voice is choked, his arms crushing me closer. I let out a sound to remind him that even though I'm dying, I still need to breathe.

His arms loosen and his glow fades, before he lifts me off him and places me gently back onto the hammock.

Holy fucking Dusk God, he just tried to fix me with his wish. That was so sweet.

He turns and strides towards the water, which is now bathed in glorious golden light, creating the perfect backdrop for the masterpiece that is Drake and making my inner whore want to lick him all over. His broad back is all coiled muscle, roaming down to his tapered waistline that would be perfect for throwing my legs around if I had the fucking energy. Too bad orgasms are off the menu because my vagina's a thirsty tart right now, and even my beast has an eye cracked open over there in the corner.

Kal flashes right next to me, giving me such a fright I almost pee my panties. He reaches down to scoop me up. "Come, Dell. We have an idea."

I push him away. "I'm not going anywhere! I've become attached to my pity island and I intend to die here. Besides, look at that pretty sunset!" I gesture to all that golden glory over there.

Sol flashes next to Kal and I'm assaulted by his hard, orgasmic glare. "You're not fucking dying. Get in his arms."

Drake unfurls his wings, pumping them once to launch into the air, coming down firmly on the other side of my hammock and sending sand spraying from here to the goddamn stars and back. "No. Not fucking happening."

Sol hisses at him like a feral cat. "Did your way work? Because she doesn't fucking look healed."

Drake glares at him, saying nothing, though his hand comes down firmly around my arm. Sol's eyes follow his movements seamlessly.

"Didn't fucking think so. We checked the boundaries, we should be able to get her in. Aero's just checking the Bright now because it might be safer to take her through there. There must be a reason it's so well guarded, and he always smells fucking terrible. It has to be where he's gaining all his extra power from."

Drake frowns. "I'm all for doing whatever we can to save her, but we can't control the situation. What if something happens to her? The King is all of her worst nightmares rolled into one."

Kal shakes his head. "She's dying, Drake. My hold on her is slipping and I know yours is too. This is our last option …"

Aero arrives next to Drake and gives them a tight nod, before they look down at me at the same fucking time.

"Move me off this island and I'll castrate the lot of you, then turn your severed cocks into petrified sex toys."

Kal smirks. "Not if you're asleep, doll."

Fucking cu—

I rouse to the smell of Satan's colon mixed with fermented shit and a little bit of dog's hairy ball sacks. Strangely, I recognise the smell, and I'm gagging before I even have a chance to open my eyes. When I do, I see a small pond dusted with a layer of decimated, rolling fog fringed with droopy trees, long tendrils of slime clinging to their spindly branches.

Though it's not a fucking pond at all; it's a bog of rolling mud, alive and bubbling, sending shit smelling particles flying into the air and enriching my senses with the smell of rotting arsehole.

"What the shit …" I'm too stunned to even try and squirm out of Kal's arms as a hand clamps over my mouth; that doesn't stop me from saying my fucking piece though. "You took me away from my perfect little death paradise and brought me to the world's fucking arsehole? Whose bright idea was this?"

"Take her clothes off," Sol orders from where he stands on a clump of moss-covered ground. He's barely escaping the bog particles flying through the air like shit arrows. I squirm, because my hackles are tingling, and there's no way I'm getting naked in this shit joint!

My body freezes, and my mouth clamps shut.

God-fucking-damnit.

I give Sol the biggest fucking death stare I can conjure for compelling me *again.* I can't wait to cut him a new arsehole.

"If this doesn't work, she's going to fucking hate us," Drake whispers, helping Aero work me out of my shift. That perked my ears, and I let it be known as I try to yell through my closed mouth.

I'm naked in Kal's arms, really confused and trying not to vomit into my mouth that has a serious case of Sol induced lockjaw.

"Hurry up and get it over with, we don't have much time before you have to initiate night," Sol growls.

"You think I don't know that?" Kal hisses, walking me towards this pit of the world's coagulated bowel excretions.

I realise what the fuck's going on—they're about to toss me into that shit bog that smells worse than something that died ten times over then was left to ferment for a year.

Fuck my life, how did I end up here.

"Take your hold off her body, Sol, or she'll sink to the bottom like a rock."

Fucking hell. These dicks. But sure enough, I can move again. The first thing I do is try to sink my nails into Kal. "Don't you fucking dar—"

He throws me.

Plop.

They're all shit listed for life, never to enjoy the bounty of my vagina because they threw me into a bog of *crap*.

Bastards.

Actually ...

Now I'm a bit distracted, because although I'm sinking into the rancid bowels of the world, my body starts to tingle all over as my skin seems to absorb whatever the hell this shit is. If I smell like the inside of a colon for the rest of my dying days, then someone's going to lose some testicles.

The sensation thickens, working its way through my body before I feel it literally start to peel away at my fucking scars. The ones on my arms, the ones on my face, the new ones on my back ... the ones I've spent the past nineteen years ignoring. It tries to tear at the one on my stomach, but I scream at the rancid fucking bog, telling the bitch to leave it alone. Ima' own that scar.

It takes the one on my hand while I'm distracted, and part of me actually mourns the loss of it.

Then my body arches as I feel something prodding at my back ... and the sensation is all too familiar because I have a fantastic fucking memory that forgets *nothing*.

No.

Fucking.

Way.

I'm not sure how this is possible, but it's fucking *happening*.

That pressure is growing, expanding as the intrusive fuckers forge their way through my back muscles that have grown over the ridges there, piercing through the skin and wounds that have long since healed.

This cannot be happening.

I feel the bastards stretch out through the bog ...

Fucking fuck-cake.

My Gods are going to hate me. Or spank me silly. Hopefully more of option B and less of option A.

I try to suck them back in ... how do these fuckers work? I could never control them when I was little; they used to pop in and out at will, knocking shit over and catching things on fire, then I lost the bastards and that was the end of that. They feel a *lot* bigger now than they were back then ...

I can't go to the fucking surface with these things out! I wonder how long I can last immersed in a shit bog without breathing? I think it just healed me of my cancer, so surely it's not going to suffocate me?

Something grabs at my shoulders and I groan, trying my best to haul my immortality granting wings in and gaining no goddamn glory, though I'm not sure I should really suck them back in when they're covered in the world's bowel remnants. I might get a wing infection. Is that a thing? I need a 'wing care crash course'.

I'm hauled over the edge of the bog and onto hard packed ground, covered from head to toe ... to wing tip ... in shit.

Wiping at my face, gagging from the overpowering stench, I flick some of the crap onto the ground in front of me.

"What. The. Fuck," Aero growls.

All four stare, like I just grew two giant penises from my back. Or wings.

I look over my shoulder at them, flopping around uselessly. Yeah, they're a lot bigger than they used to be. The last time I saw the bastards they were so tiny and cute. Now they're all long and elegant. And dirty. Really fucking dirty ...

"Follow me," Sol snaps, reaching down and grabbing my arm. He's looking at me like he wants to cut a hoe.

They all grab onto him and we flash through the Bright, onto his secret island that's all golden from the sinking dawn.

But I don't get a chance to appreciate the beauty and sea

air, as Kal and Sol grab me under my armpits, one on each side, and half drag me towards the fucking water, my wings trailing us along the sand.

It's about now I really start to panic. "No! No, no, no… don't you fucking dare! I'll eat your fucking testicles!" Yeah, they aren't listening to me. Although my wings are fucking filthy, at this point, I'd be more than happy for them to be caked in shit forever. The repercussions of the alternative are too severe for me to stomach right now …

I look at Drake and Aero following behind us, looking fucking murderous. And sexy, even though they're speckled in the same shit I'm caked from head to toe in. I wonder momentarily if I'm going to smell like a toilet for the rest of my newly reclaimed immortal life, because I was essentially re-born in a pool of shit?

Fucking hope not.

"Please, Drake, don't let them toss me in!"

He ignores me. Wanker. "You guys are about as helpful as a pair of floppy penises!"

But then Kal lets go of my arm, which Sol then grabs, and I'm lifted off the ground as my angry Day God propels us into the air.

"Tuck them in, Dell." I do as he asks, even though he isn't compelling me, because I know what's fucking coming.

He flicks his wings twice, hauling me past the shallows, then releases me.

I go 'plop' for the second time today.

Bastards. They're all shit listed for the rest of my immortal life. And I'm *definitely* going to stop fantasising about having their penises inside me.

The water's swirling, muddied by the brown shit that's washing off me, hiding me from the predators. I don't mean the malicious creatures that lurk in the depths of the ocean.

I'm talking about the predators that hunt my weakness within—exposing all my lacking to the world.

And I'm running out of breath.

I refuse to go to the surface ... to shed the muddy mask on my reality. Right now, I'm more naked, more vulnerable than I've ever been before.

How the fuck do these bastards work? I scrunch my face up, trying desperately to suck them back in, but it's like having a penis prodded into your anus; it goes against your arse grain. In short, it's a lot easier to get them *out* than it is to pull them back *in*. Something I learnt the hard way ... all those years ago.

A rogue wave surges me back, then flicks me forward so quickly I'm sucking in a breath of water as I'm hurled towards the beach like a feathery fucking catapult, where I land at the feet of my four Sun Gods, choking and spluttering, my pure white fucking wings splayed hopelessly around me.

Regaining my limited composure, I look up at them. Is it the fading light, or are they all about ten shades paler than they usually are?

They certainly don't look like they're in the mood for some light hearted spanking.

Damn ...

"Surprise?"

No answer.

Not everyone likes surprises, I guess.

The end of book two.

ACKNOWLEDGMENTS

Thank you, Mum and Dad. You are a pillar of support and have always urged me to follow my dreams. I never expected those dreams would compel me to write a story about a prostitute who has conversations with her vagina, but we'll ignore that finer detail. I know you are proud of me, and that's all that matters!

Mum, when I read you the first chapter of book one of this series, you never once batted an eyelid at all the slippery vaginas, never once told me I should write something more pertinent. In fact, you proceeded to sit down and brainstorm the rest of the series with me while we laughed hysterically over highly inappropriate innuendo.

Thank you for making me feel validated every day of my life. Thank you for the countless hours you have spent helping me to polish my work. I couldn't have done this without you.

My darling husband - thank you for believing in me, for reminding me of my untapped potential ... I bet you never expected it would spurt onto the pages of a book in the form of a reverse harem, huh?! (Insert laughing face here) But in all seriousness, thank you for sticking it out with me.

Nana, thank you for inspiring me with your creativity, and for showing me how strong and independent a woman can be. I love you, and not a day goes by that I don't miss you.

Lauren, thank you for the hours you invested into helping me, not to mention holding my hand through the entire publishing process. Most importantly, thank you for laughing at my vulgar sense of humour and dishing it right back at me.

My amazing BETA group, thank you all for investing time into this series, and giving me such validation. You're all wonderful.

To everyone else who has supported me along this journey that has only just begun, thank you!

ABOUT THE AUTHOR

SARAH ASHLEIGH PARKER

Sarah is New Zealand born and lives in the Gold Coast, Australia with her husband and their three children. She discovered her love for the written word early on, devouring book after book and creating her own stories in her spare time, winning various competitions throughout her school years for her quirky imagination.

It's only recently that she has been able to fully immerse herself into writing, being at home with three young children and an unquenchable thirst for creativity.

And so, with the timing being as good as it ever gets, and the passion and determination of a woman possessed, Sarah threw herself into becoming an author. Juggling an eclectic mix of manic writing, editing and proofing sessions, child rearing, homemaking and everything else life throws around, she somehow makes it work.

Sarah's preferred genre is adult fantasy romance and contemporary romance.

SPAWN OF DARKNESS SERIES

A Token's Worth
A Feather's Worth
A Lover's Worth
A Woman's Worth

A
LOVER'S
WORTH

Spawn of Darkness

S.A. PARKER